Devoted
TO THE ENEMY

VENTURI MAFIA BOOK 3

NIKKI ROSE

Copyright © 2023 Nikki Rose.

All rights reserved. No part of this publication may be reproduced, distributed, or transmitted in any form or by any means, including photocopying, recording, or other electronic or mechanical methods, without the prior written permission of the publisher, except in the case of brief quotations embodied in critical reviews and certain other noncommercial uses permitted by copyright law.

.

Any references to historical events, real people, or real places are used fictitiously. Names, characters, and places are products of the author's imagination.

Book design by Nikki Rose.

First printing edition 2023.

All rights reserved.

ISBN: 9798372515246

Venturi Mafia Reading Order

CONTENTS

CHAPTER 1

Mia

'Teo, what happened?'

'Some guy just sideswiped my car.'

'Are you okay?'

'Yeah, but he—fuck.' There was a loud crashing sound, followed by something that sounded similar to a rock tumbler before the line went dead.

'Teo? Teo?' I yelled into the phone, but the line had disconnected.

"Mia?" Gabe's voice snapped, bringing me back. We have to go, *now*."

"Okay just let me call Mira and let her know what's going on." I opened my phone's lock screen and started to scroll when Gabe jerked it out of my hand.

"Gabe, what the hell?" I glared up at him, but my anger turned to shock as he pulled a gun from his pocket and pointed it at me. I stumbled backward, stuttering over my words. "What's going on? Where's Teo?"

"You need to worry less about Teo and more about yourself. Even now you're so blinded by him that he's all you can think of. You're not even worried about the fact that I could shoot you right now and you'd be dead?"

"Okay. I'm sorry. But I'm confused. What's going on?"

"What's going on is you're going to quit asking stupid questions and walk out of here with me right now or I'm going to shoot you and anyone that gets in my way. Do you understand?"

My eyes widened as I took in everything he was saying. I knew that Gabe had made mistakes in the past, but I had no idea that he had this in him. I held my hands up in front of me to try to show him that I wasn't a threat and hopefully calm him down.

"I understand. Please don't hurt me or anyone else. I'll go."

"Good. Now, come on." Gabe motioned toward the door with a slight jerk of the gun, and I moved. "Put your hands down and act natural. If I even think someone's suspicious, I'll start shooting."

"Okay. Okay. I'm going."

My heart pounded in my ears and my hands shook at my sides as I walked through the bustling house filled with caterers, florists, and a few early wedding guests.

Gabe led me down the back stairs and through the downstairs pantry, toward the back door.

"Mia, Mia!" Courtney called to me, and I held my breath as I turned to her with a forced smile.

"Hey, Courtney. What's up?" I tried my best to keep my voice calm and even.

"We're supposed to be meeting the photographer in five minutes at the front stairs. What are you doing?"

"I just need to take care of something really quick. I'll be right there." I struggled to give her a convincing smile, but Courtney didn't seem to notice my nervousness, or if she did she may have excused it as wedding jitters.

Courtney smiled. "Okay I'll see you there. I still can't believe you're getting married today."

"I know." I smiled excitedly but inside my heart was breaking. I suspected that if Gabe had his way, I wouldn't be getting married at all.

Gabe nudged me with the gun in his pocket, urging me to wrap up the conversation.

"I better hurry so that I don't keep the photographer waiting too long."

"Okay. See you there," Courtney said cheerfully as she hurried on her way, and Gabe led me out the back door.

The vineyard was beautiful, set up with wooden chairs and gold ribbon that marked the aisle between two rows of grape vines. An elegant, understated arch of white and cream colored flowers stood on a small rise where Teo and I were supposed to say our vows in just under an hour.

Gabe grabbed my arm and yanked me away to the side of the house where a black SUV waited. He opened the back door and shoved me inside, slamming the door shut before I had a chance to right myself.

I waited until Gabe put some distance between us as he rounded the car to the driver side, and I grabbed for the door handle, but it was locked. I struggled with the latch, but it must have had child safety locks on it because the door wouldn't open.

I screamed and banged on the window. Gabe tensed, looking back at me then around the yard to make sure no one heard anything just before hands stretched out from the third row of seating, covering my face with a rag that made my head spin. Just as I was about to lose consciousness I felt a sharp prick at the side of my neck and the world went dark.

Teo

One minute I was driving along, talking to Mia, heading toward my wedding with my whole life ahead of me, the next my car was flipping on its side and rolling down the steep ravine. I wasn't sure what came over me but as the car rolled, I leaped from the car into the thick brush.

My ears rang and my head pounded but I knew I had made the right choice when my car landed at the bottom of the ravine and burst into a fiery explosion that shook the ground beneath me.

I wasn't sure if whoever had run me off the road would come back around and make sure that the job was done, so I reached for my gun, but it was no longer at my side where I always kept it. It had probably fallen during the crash along with my cell phone that I vaguely remember flying out of my hand on impact. I scrambled, looking for the gun and finally spotted a glint of metal in the tall shrubs.

I grabbed the pistol and scrambled as best as I could into the thicker overgrowth and settled my back against a large rock.

I scrubbed my hand over my face. My whole body hurt, and my mind felt groggy, but I had to focus. I waited for several minutes until I was sure that whoever drove me off the road wasn't coming back. Chances were that they saw the explosion and assumed that I was burning down below.

Whoever it was that had tried to kill me was bold, I'd give them that. But they were also stupid because I survived. I would find whoever it was that tried to take me out and make them suffer.

I stumbled, struggling to find my footing as I pushed myself to my feet. I kept close to the upward slope and leaned on it for balance, grateful for the fairly level ledge that broke my fall.

I couldn't climb the steep hill where my car had gone over, especially not without any climbing gear, so instead, I limped my way parallel to the road above until the slope tapered off.

The level ground made walking easier, but my ankle still hurt anytime I put pressure on it. Experience told me that it probably wasn't broken, just a bad sprain. In either case, I didn't need to be walking on it, but I couldn't trust hitchhiking and risk running into someone who worked for whoever drove me off the road. I had my suspicions of who might be motivated to stop the wedding from happening. I would be sure to hunt down whoever was responsible just as soon as I made it home safely and married the love of my life.

I had walked about a mile when a dark sports car came down the road. I ducked behind some overgrowth, but they had already seen me and pulled over to the side of the road. I gripped my gun until my knuckles ached and prepared myself in case it was someone coming to finish the job.

"Teo? Is that you?" Alessandro's voice called out from the other side of the shrubs and my shoulders sagged with relief.

I stumbled my way out of the brush, and he rushed to my side, grabbing my arm to help pull me up onto the side of the road.

"Man, I'm glad to see you."

"What the hell happened to you?"

Another two cars came flying down the road, slamming on brakes and pulling over to see what was going on. Nic drove one car with Enzo in the passenger seat while Luca and Dario were in the other.

"Hey, what's going—*shit*. Teo, you okay?" Nic asked through his window.

"We're good," Alessandro said. "Go on ahead. I'm going to get him checked out then we'll catch up."

"Okay I'll text you with whatever I find."

Nic and the other car drove away, and I looked at Alessandro suspiciously.

"What's going on? Where are they headed? The vineyards the other way."

"They're not heading to the vineyard, and neither are we."

A sinking washed over me when I looked at Alessandro's expression. "What happened?"

"First we need to get you taken care of. Then I'll explain everything."

"Explain first," I challenged.

"Okay but remember you're no good to anyone hurt and beat up like this and if you have a concussion you

7

need to be seen before you run off trying to play superhero."

"I think we both know I'm no hero." I raised my brow and waited expectantly. "What's wrong?"

"It's Mia," Alessandro said hesitantly. "She's missing."

"Missing? What the hell do you mean she's missing? Where did she go?"

"If I knew that she wouldn't be missing," Alessandro said flatly. "I'll explain everything on the way to get you help."

"No, I'm not going anywhere except to find Mia."

"Teo, that place on your head doesn't look good and I saw you limping. You need to have your foot and your head looked at before you go off searching for her. The guys are on it and they're going to keep me updated."

"I'm not wasting time getting looked at until after I find Mia."

"Look, you may be my future don. But you're also one of my best friends, so right now I'm going to tell you like it is. You're going to go get checked out and make sure that you're okay. Then, we're going to find Mia together. We will catch up with the guys as soon as you're taken care of but for now, you're going to get in my car and I'm going to take you to get looked at by the doc."

"Alessandro..." I growled but he didn't back down.

"You'll get there a lot faster in my car than you will trying to hobble along to catch up to the other guys."

8

I let Alessandro lead me to his car and reluctantly climbed inside. Once we were flying down the road in the opposite direction the guys had gone. I glanced over at him begrudgingly.

"You do realize that this could be seen as insubordination right?"

"Yeah, well, you can scold me later. Right now, we need to get you taken care of and find your girl."

.

CHAPTER 2

Mia

I jolted awake from a sudden movement that jarred my entire body. It seemed too sudden and was gone too fast to be an earthquake, but I sat up straight and glanced around the dark room.

There was barely any light seeping through what appeared to be seams in the corners of the walls. I wasn't sure where I was, and my head felt like it was filled with thick mud. I rubbed my eyes, trying to get the film away and blinked a few times, but I still couldn't see much with the low lighting.

I stumbled to my feet, feeling as if the whole room was rocking back and forth. I barely made it to the wall without falling over and reached out to hold myself up.

The walls were metal and crimped like what you would see in a storage building or a shipping container. As I held on to the wall I realized that the rocking motion, while intensified by whatever I'd been drugged with, was not all in my head.

I held on to the wall and made my way to where the light seemed to come in the most around the door to the shipping container I assumed I was in, but it wouldn't budge. I bang my fist on the door and called out even though my throat felt like sandpaper. I had a feeling that my chance of someone hearing me was slim.

After screaming for what seemed like a long time, but was probably only minutes, the door opened and a man I didn't recognize walked through.

"Who are you?" I stepped back, realizing that making a fuss was probably not the best idea. "Where are we? Where are you taking me?"

"So many questions," he said with slight amusement as he stepped toward me slowly and I stumbled backward, losing my footing and falling back onto the hard metal floor. Pain shot through my wrist and shoulder on impact.

"Be careful. You're going to end up hurting yourself. Here let me help you up." He spoke in a light tone that made me think that he wasn't the one who had originally taken me and probably had no distinctive ill will toward me. Most likely I was just another job to him and at least he seemed like he didn't want me harmed. He reached down and I let him help me up.

"Here, let me see that." He gently took my wrist in his large hand and carefully felt around to examine my

11

injury. "It doesn't seem to be broken but you have to be careful, at least until you get your sea legs. It's hard to walk on a ship even at the best of times and I'm sorry to say but this isn't yours."

"Please can you help me? I don't know what I'm doing here. I don't know who took me. Can you give me some answers? Can you help me, please?" I grabbed a hold of his arm, pleading with him desperately. "If it's money you're after, I can pay you whatever they're paying, plus more. I'll double it, triple it even. I have money. My fiancé has money. And I know he will pay a lot to have me returned safely to him."

"I don't think your fiancé is going to be much help to you now and as for you, you'll find out all the answers you're looking for soon enough."

The coolness of his voice and the uncaring numbness in his eyes made me realize that the man before me was not my ally. He was not going to help me. I started to pull my hand away from his arm, but his other hand struck out like a viper, gripping my wrist like a vise. Before I knew what was happening, he spun me around so that my back was to his front, his arm restraining me across my chest. I struggled against him but soon a familiar prick on the side of my neck caused my whole body to go limp, and I blacked out again.

When I woke up again, I was no longer in the shipping container, and we were no longer moving. I felt like I had been asleep for days. My body was stiff and sore, and my eyes practically stuck together.

I fought through the grogginess, taking my time and moving slowly to open my eyes. The room was better lit but that offered me little comfort when I looked around at what appeared to be a prison cell built into an old wine cellar.

I had no idea how much time had passed or what had happened during that time, but my head ached, and my mouth was dry.

"Good, you're finally awake. I thought maybe my man had given you too much tranquilizer and that you might never wake up." The familiar voice sent an eerie chill down my spine. "That would be quite a shame considering how much work I went through to get you here." *Andrea*.

"You? What happened? What did you do?" A sudden memory of being in my bedroom, looking at myself in the mirror in my white wedding dress flashed in my mind. I remembered the phone call with Teo, someone walking into my room, shattered glass on the floor. *Gabe.* Gabe had taken me. But why? He worked for Teo, not the Romanos.

"Gabe? Gabe gave me to you?"

Andrea chuckled. "You Monticellis and Venturis are so much alike. You think someone is just going to blindly be loyal to you no matter what you do to them. You are just that wonderful that everyone is going to bow down to you even when you treat them unfairly. Yes, Gabe gave you to me and all it took was me promising a higher station in my family then your fiancé was willing to give."

"But why? Teo spared him."

"Spared him?" Andrea laughed bitterly. "He showed him complete disrespect by dropping his rank down to nothing more than security at a strip club. That was pathetic. Gabe is proving to me that he could be a very good asset for my family, and I reward those who do well for me and my family."

"Where are we?"

"We're in Corsica," he said calmly. "You see, I learned my lesson last time. Your fiancé's reach was a little further than what I had expected but this time I have anticipated every possible scenario and you won't be getting away from me so easily this time."

"So, what? You're going to keep me here until I make a choice again? I'll never choose to be your wife. Ever."

"That's where I made a mistake before. I shouldn't have given you a choice. You see, this time there is no choice. You will become my wife sooner or later and until you do you will stay here with me under lock and key. Last time I made things too comfortable for you, a nice soft bed and fancy dinners. I showed you respect when you deserve none. You see, the one main mistake that I made last time was that I treated you as someone who would make a logical decision when given the options to do so. What I forgot was that just because you were given a high station by your father to lead his empire, you're still just a woman."

"Just a woman?" I didn't try to hide my offense.

"Yes and I also realized something else since the last time we were together. Breaking in a wife and breaking in a slave is not much different. You will not be given luxuries and comforts unless you earn them. And I will break you. Once you're broken then we will be married and hopefully then you will know your place as my wife."

Fear gripped me around the throat and threatened to strangle me.

"Now, come on. There's something I want you to see." Andrea unlocked the cage and motioned for me to come to him.

When I didn't move, he stepped into the cell with me, making the space feel even smaller than it had. He roughly grabbed my hair and pulled me from the cell. I clawed at his hand, trying to break free, but it was no use as I stumbled down the cobblestone hallway. We passed through a doorway and into a large open ballroom that had seen better days. Inside were several people, mostly men and a few women who were obviously there against their will as they stood there eyes down like beaten dogs.

Andrea forced my head up to look out among the people. "All these people work for me. Every last one of them is loyal to me and in case they aren't or in case they have any second thoughts about it we are here today to erase any doubt they might have. This will also act as a way for you to see that you have no allies here. You have no friends, and no one is going to help you this time. Bring him out." Andrea yelled to someone off to the side. A moment later there was a sound of scuffling and Gianni was forced through a door by two large men who held him on either shoulder, his hands tied behind his back.

"This man tried to help this woman once before. Not because he was looking out for her, granted, it was for money which I can respect, but he went against me and that can't happen. In case any of you have any thoughts or crisis of conscience about possibly helping *Signora* Monticelli, hopefully this will erase any doubt from your mind." Andrea lifted a gun in his hand and pointed at

15

Gianni. I screamed out as the bullet shot from the gun, landing square between Gianni's eyes, sending him crumpling to the ground at Andrea's feet.

"This is what happens to anyone who tries to help her in any way. Next time it will be long, drawn out, and painful instead of quick and painless.

There was a quiet roar among the people as they began chattering quietly but I couldn't make out what anyone was saying. All I could do was stand there, staring at Gianni's body, while blood pooled under his head.

I was in a foreign country without an ally in sight and now any potential ally had just been threatened with death if they even tried to help me. My situation was bleak, and I had no idea if or when Teo would ever be able to find me or how I might escape on my own, but I knew that somehow, some way, I had to.

CHAPTER 3

Teo

I sat in my father's parlor, downing my third whiskey in hopes that it would help drown out the pain. I hadn't slept at all in two days, and I barely managed a couple of hours here and there in the week that Mia had been missing. Even in my grief-stricken state I knew that I needed sleep if I was going to think and act clearly and find Mia before something terrible happened. Whoever was responsible for her abduction had gotten Gabe to take her, so chances were that they wanted her alive but for how long I wasn't sure.

And even if they planned on keeping her alive indefinitely there was no telling what Mia was going through.

My sleep deprived mind wandered back to the moment I found out that Mia had been taken.

"Okay, I'm in the car, we're headed back to let a doctor take a look at me, now tell me what happened." I looked to Alessandro, demanding answers.

"Okay, but I need you to stay calm. And remember you gave me your word that you would get checked out before we do anything to find Mia. You're no good to her if you keel over in the process."

"I gave you my word now tell me what's going on?"

Alessandro had taken a deep breath before beginning. *"Everything was going smoothly and was on track for the wedding. The girls talked to Mia about a half an hour before she went missing. They were supposed to be meeting at the front stairway to have their photo taken and Mia asked for a few minutes alone. A little while later, Courtney saw Mia and Gabe coming down the back stairs near the kitchen. Mia told Courtney that she would be there in a few minutes for the photos, and that she just had to take care of something first, but Courtney said that she didn't seem overly anxious, and she just chocked it up to pre-wedding jitters."*

"Mia has always been calm under pressure," I said with a hint of admiration in my voice. For someone who hadn't grown up familiar with the life that we live, Mia had a way about her. She was able to stay calm in the face of danger in the face of threats, she could think, and act as poised as someone who had been raised their whole life to prepare them.

"So, either she didn't know that she was in danger, or she didn't have a choice. If that son of a bitch did anything—"

"Don't go there," Alessandro had said firmly. *"The guys are already out chasing down leads. Luca and Dario are heading to the club to question people that worked with Gabe to see if they have any idea who he might have been involved with or if he started acting strange over the past few weeks. We've got our guys at the airports and docks keeping an eye out for her."*

"Good. I want to question Courtney myself since she was the only one to see the two of them together. We need to have the Monticelli security team start pulling footage and see if they can piece together anything. Dante's already got someone on that. I'm not sure who we can trust anymore. We need to keep our circle tight and make sure that we don't make any mistakes like we did with Gabe. Speaking of, get me his wife. I need to have a chat with her as well."

"I figured you might. Nick and Enzo are on their way to pick her up now. They'll be meeting us back at the vineyard."

"The vineyard? Why not the compound?"

"The vineyard's where it happened so, I figured that it would be best if we stay around there just in case it helps jog anyone's memory or we find any new evidence."

"Sounds like you've really got a handle on things. Thank you for your help."

"It's no problem at all you know I'd do anything to help you and the family."

"I'm going to call my guys and see if they can hack into the traffic cams around where the accident happened. I want to see who ran me off the road and if they could possibly be connected with Gabe and Mia's disappearance. The timing of both of these attacks is something more than a coincidence. This was a planned attack."

I'd spent the next week scouring every corner of Northern Italy. I spread the word to the Monticellis and

Venturis to search both of our territories and sent teams of my men led by those that I trusted most to all the other major cities and towns but the main person I was focused on was Andrea. He had taken her once before, and I had no doubt that he could have been the one who took her again.

My men and I raided the Romano compound but there had been no sign of Mia or Andrea. I'd called in every favor I had, every ally, anyone that I could bribe. I even called the senator to get him to pull strings with the authorities to try to find Mia. I was desperate and running out of leads.

A knock on the Parlor door drew my attention from my thoughts and I irritably called out, "come in."

Lucia walked in looking as weary as I felt. She was close to Mia, and I hadn't even considered that she was probably going through hell worrying about her and there she was having to work. I needed to give her time off. Bianca and the other housekeepers could pick up the slack. The only reason Lucia was even working there was to have someone that Mia was comfortable with.

"Yes, Lucia. What is it?"

"I'm sorry to bother you, sir. There's someone wishing to see you."

"Why didn't the guards contact me?"

"They didn't want to bother you, so they asked me instead."

"So, my guards are a bunch of cowards that don't want to bother me? They would rather send a woman to do it, huh? Have I become that unbearable?"

20

"Of course not, sir. We're all worried about Mia. I mean *Signora* Monticelli.

"Who is it that wants to see me?"

"Isabella Salvatore."

"I don't know anyone by that name."

"She says that she has some information that may be helpful to you."

"Send her in." I held my breath as Lucia escorted a pretty young woman into the parlor. While it was clear that she was beautiful, there was a certain weariness that aged her.

"You are Isabella, I presume." I said as she came closer, and I motioned for her to sit. "I'm told that you have some information for me but first, who are you?"

"I believe you know my husband, Gianni Salvatore."

"Gianni? He works for Romano," I said coolly.

"Gianni told me that he helped you when your girl was taken by Andrea Romano."

"Yes he helped me—for a price, of course. But why are you here now?"

"Gianni told me that he was going on a special assignment with Andrea and that he wouldn't be back for several months. Once I heard news of Mia Monticelli's disappearance, I knew that the two had to be connected."

"And why should I believe you? Why should I think that you are any different than any other person who is acquainted with Romano? Why would I believe a word out of your mouth?"

"I believe that Gianni is dead," she blurted out.

"Dead? Why do you think that?"

"Because Gianni was paranoid. We had specific check-in times that he would text me, no matter what, with certain key phrases so that I knew that everything was all right. He's missed the last two check-ins."

"And you think that that's enough to risk coming to see me? You think that he's dead just because he didn't check in with you twice?"

"He has never missed one in the ten years that we have been together—not one."

"And why come to me?" I found myself growing increasingly irritated with her. I had my own problems that I needed to deal with.

"Gianni told me that you are an honorable man—more honorable than him or any of the Romanos. He told me that he had helped you once and that if anything were to happen to him that I was to come to you and request safety and protection."

"Gianni didn't do me any favors. He did a job, and I paid him for it. I don't owe him or you anything."

"I know, but Gianni said that you were an honorable man and that you would do right and help anyway."

"Why should I trust anything that you're saying?"

"When a man in your organization dies, what happens to his widow? To his children?"

I looked at her curiously, wondering where she was going with her line of questioning.

"We take care of them. We make sure that they have a roof over their heads and food on the table. If the children are young then we help support the young mother until the children are old enough to go off to school, at which point we help her find a job within one of our many businesses so that she can earn a living for her and her children."

"Do you know what they do to widows and children of the fallen men in the Romano family?" I shook my head and her eyes dropped to the floor for a moment before she looked back up at me with steel in her spine and ice in her veins. "They sell them. Attractive widows go to the sex trade, older or unattractive ones are put to work as indentured servants, the children work cleaning houses or doing whatever chores they can until they determine where they will go and what sort of training they will have.

"Gianni did not love me. I was not his wife because he loved me. I was his wife because he owned me, and I got pregnant. He didn't want our child to be born a bastard, so he married me. There is no love lost between us. But Gianni did love our daughter and he was afraid for her if something happened to him. That's why he told me to do this, to come to you, and to beg you to protect me and her if something were to happen to him. They will sell her off the moment they get their hands on her. We've been staying with relatives, trying to hide until I could get to you as soon as he missed the first check-in."

"How old is your daughter?" I asked with a more tender tone.

"She's nine. Andrea had already been eyeing her. He would make little comments that he passed off his jokes about how beautiful she was and how much money she would bring when she was of age. He won't hesitate to rip my daughter from my arms and sell her to the highest bidder. Do what you want with me, but I am begging you to protect her. If you agree, I will give you everything that I know about where they took Mia and what Andrea's plan is."

"I didn't think that Gianni told you the full plan."

"He didn't, but his computer did. When he missed the first check-in I hacked his computer and went through all his records. Even his text messages are backed up onto that thing. He didn't know that I knew the password, but it was easy to figure out over time. Being with someone for ten years, you get to know them pretty well."

"All right. I will protect you and your daughter. I won't let Romano harm you in any way. You are under my protection. Now tell me what you know."

CHAPTER 4

Mia

Despair. Pure and utter despair. There was no other word to describe the way I felt after being thrown back into my cell by one of Andrea's men.

I sat there numb for a while on the hard stone floor.

I was in a foreign country, surrounded by enemies on all sides, with no means of escape. Teo would search all of Italy for me. He might even look as far as Sicily, but there was no way that he would think to look in Corsica. There would be no reason for him to. We hadn't heard anything out of the Corsicans since they left him for dead in the south of France.

Teo. There was some memory there that I couldn't quite recall, something that I needed to remember that lingered just out of reach. I closed my eyes and thought back to the last memory that I had before I was taken. Flashes of memories popped in my head. The champagne glass shattered to the floor as I turned to see Gabe standing in my room. Before that...I forced my brain to think back further.

'The photographer wants us all to meet at the main staircase to start pictures in about fifteen minutes.' Courtney's voice echoed in my mind, and I saw her standing in my doorway, smiling.

I'd taken a nervous breath, my eyes wide in the mirror as I peered back at myself in my mother's wedding dress. *'You guys mind giving me a few minutes to myself?'*

'Not at all.' Vittoria smiled softly before leaving the room.

'Not getting cold feet, I hope,' I heard Teo's voice in my head as the memories grew choppy.

'I can't wait to marry you,' I smiled to myself as I remembered the moment.

'Me neither. Then you will officially be mine and we can start enjoying our life—shit.'

My heart began to race as the memories came faster in quick flashes.

'Some guy just sideswiped my car.'

'Are you okay?'

26

'Yeah, but he—fuck.*'* There had been a loud crashing sound, followed by something that sounded like a rock tumbler before the line went dead.

'Teo? Teo?' I yelled into the phone, but the line had disconnected.

Trembling, I drew my knees up to my chest and allowed myself a few minutes to fall apart, hiding my face and letting the tears flow.

There I'd been, wondering if there was any way that Teo might think to look for me in Corsica when I didn't even know if he was alive. Someone had sideswiped him but that sounded a lot worse than a little fender bender. The timing of the accident was suspicious as well and made me wonder if it wasn't an organized attack to keep him from being able to come find me. I felt sick at the realization that something bad could have happened to Teo. Violent sobs constricted my chest, making it hard to breathe. I had to get a hold of myself. I forced myself to take in a deep breath, holding it for a few seconds before blowing it out slowly. After a few more minutes of repeating those steps, I'd barely been able to calm myself enough that I was only snubbing when my tears were quickly halted by the sound of footsteps growing louder. Someone was coming my direction. I quickly wiped away my tears and held my breath.

"Oh, don't stop your crying on my account. I don't mind them. On the contrary, I plan to revel in them before we're done." Andrea's voice was cold and cruel.

I climbed to my feet and cleared my throat, trying to put some strength behind my words as I rose from the floor and straightened my back. "You're wasting your time. I will never marry you."

27

Andrea looked at me the way one might look at an errant child who had just said something ridiculous.

"Look at you. So strong willed, so brave." His voice was mocking. "You will marry me, eventually. But we're not there yet. We have quite a way to go to break you down before you'll be ready to be my wife."

I took a step back in the cell needing to add a small bit of distance between Andrea and myself no matter how futile that was when I was locked in that stupid cage. He motioned to someone outside of my view and a moment later another man stepped over to the iron bars and started to unlock the door.

He didn't say a word, but his presence made me nervous, and I took another step back.

"What's going on?"

The man stepped into the cell, looked at me with cold expressionless eyes, and back at Andrea who nodded.

"My mother always said that a man should never lay a hand on his wife in anger. So Ciro is going to handle that for me."

"W-what?" I stepped back as the man came closer.

"You look far too comfortable in this cell like this so we're going to have to do something about that." He looked from me to Ciro.

"Remove her clothes. She doesn't get anything until she earns it."

"What? No." I yelled and swung at the man's hands as he reached for me.

"Do not resist or you will be punished," Andrea warned but I ignored him. Focused more on my present assailant.

"Strike her." I barely had time to register Andrea's bark when Ciro's hand struck hard enough across my face that I fell to the floor.

I sobbed, cupping my face, and struggling against double vision for a moment.

"I warned you," Andrea said calmly. "Maybe being strung up for a while will help take some of the fight out of her."

The man still never said a word as he grabbed me roughly. I fought in vain as he forced my hands up over my head, tugging down a pair of shackles I hadn't noticed hanging high above my head.

I squirmed and tried to fight him off, but it was no use. With my hands bound above my head, I had to stand on my tiptoes to keep the pressure of my weight off of my wrists.

As if that weren't bad enough. Once I was helplessly hanging there, Ciro was free to unceremoniously rip my clothes off of me, tossing the torn rags into the corner until I was hanging there, completely naked with no way to cover myself. I felt unbearably vulnerable. I wanted to hide away, to wrap my arms around myself, to shield my bare flesh from their prying eyes but there was no way.

Andrea tapped his ring against the bar of the cell once, almost sounding like a gong and without warning, Ciro struck me hard in my belly.

I cried out, instinctively pulling on the chains to try to double over but all I could do was swing there until my scrambling feet managed to gain purchase on the floor once again.

I coughed and gasped for air that had been forced from my lungs. Several moments later, there was another tapping sound and Ciro struck me again. That time, making me throw up what little I had left in my stomach.

I was barely aware of Ciro pulling a long, thin stick from outside of the cell. It whistled as it cut through the air before landing with a painful sting across my back that made me suck in a large gasp of air. He began alternating between my stomach and my back, always pausing in between just long enough that I would start to let my guard down before he'd strike again.

Andrea stepped into the cell and the man took a step back from us as Andrea roughly gripped my hair, forcing my head back so that my eyes met his.

"Had enough?"

"Please, stop this," I rasped.

"Oh, my *topolina*. We are just getting started."

He released my hair roughly, shoving my head forward and he stepped back with a swift gesture to Ciro that I was barely aware of before he barked out his command. "Again."

Ciro struck my midsection again, causing me to cry out. The pain caused me to pull on my wrists and the metal cut into my skin.

I coughed and strained for air and by the time I came to my senses, Andrea stood beside me.

"My *topolina,* you are damaging yourself," Andrea said with a tisk. He ran his finger along the searing wounds on my wrists, making them burn worse before he turned his voice to Ciro. "Go get the crate while I release her."

Relief flooded my body when he unclasped the shackles, but the moment my weight shifted to my legs, I crumpled toward the floor. The only thing that stopped me was Andrea's arms wrapping around me and holding me up.

I hated being that close to him and I wanted to shove him away and run but my body was too weak. I was vaguely aware of motion in the cell as Ciro came back inside. I struggled to move my head, hardly able to see what he was doing through the strands of hair that stuck to my sweat-dampened face.

Relief was replaced quickly by panic and a nauseating feeling in my gut as I saw the dog crate being placed near the center of the cell.

"What's that for?"

"As I said, you will earn every freedom and every comfort including the freedom to move. This small crate is just barely big enough for you to fit in, but you'll have to remain in the fetal position the whole time. It can be excruciating."

"No, please? Please don't do this." Fear and panic sent a surge of strength through my weak and battered body, and I managed to temporarily break free from Andrea's unsuspecting grasp. But that victory was short-lived as he grabbed me by the hair near my scalp and yanked me backward only releasing me so that I could sling to the ground. Pain reverberated through my entire body as I landed hard on the stone floor. Before I could recuperate, Andrea grabbed me by my hair and dragged me over to the crate.

He forced me inside and I had no choice but to assume the fetal position to be able to even fit in the metal wire crate. He slammed and locked the door shut and I sobbed as my joints already ached.

"Let me out of here. Please," I cried out, but Andrea just chuckled.

"I'll see you soon, *topolina*. A few hours like this should help soften you up a bit."

CHAPTER 5

Teo

I didn't like the idea of getting Intel from someone within Andrea's organization but after hearing Isabella's story, I believed her. I hoped that my trust in her would not be in vain. Isabella told me how she was able to access Gianni's computer and how she found plans to travel to Corsica after abducting Mia. It made sense. I had enemies in Corsica that would be willing to help other enemies of mine. After all, there was a reason for the saying the enemy of my enemy is my friend. If Andrea couldn't take me down himself, the coward would run to someone more powerful like the Corsicans. And he was right in one regard, I never would have expected it.

I hadn't given much thought to the Corsicans since we took down that team of shooters five years ago.

Memories flashed in my mind of the attack on the beach, when the men threatened to take Mia, describing all the horrible things they wanted to do to her while I watched. The thought of her being in their custody, and their country along with Andrea who was a monster in his own right, was more than I could bear. I pushed my fears out of my mind and blocked out the thoughts of what Mia might be going through at that very moment so that I could focus on getting her back. I called an emergency meeting of all the most trusted men in the organization, along with a few other capos who I knew had strong forces. I also called La Guerriglia for help. He had the largest militant group of men, loyal only to him, outside of an official Italian crime family. Best of all, he was a loyal friend to me.

If Mia had still been in Italy, I would have already stormed wherever she was being kept, shooting down anyone in my way, but traveling to another country would be tricky. Especially somewhere as tightly controlled as Corsica. It wasn't that the French government was keeping a close look on the island, but no one came into or out of Corsica without the Corsican mob knowing about it. They were well infiltrated which meant we had to be extremely careful.

Choosing the wrong entry point could mean the difference between making it to save Mia or being stopped at the port before we even stood a chance.

There were no borders to sneak across, there was only the open sea, ready to expose any vessel that headed toward its shores. We had to be extremely smart. I didn't have many contacts in France but luckily I knew someone who did. La Guerriglia was an independent mercenary who gained his nickname from his preferred fighting tactics. He had a large loyal Army of men and no official allegiance to any one crime family. Even though he did jobs for other families, he never accepted any that targeted the Venturi family. He was loyal to me, and I had been trying for years to get him to officially join us. But in Mia's case, his stubbornness to keep independent might help me.

La Guerriglia had contacts in France and Corsica with the ability to smuggle through a company of cargo ships. We had to wait two days for him to hear back from his contacts and one more for them to prepare a way for us.

The moment I got the intel on Mia, things moved very quickly. I couldn't waste any time getting her back. With men like that, I didn't know how long she had before they would break her. Memories flashed in my mind. Images of girls I had seen in the past broken, beaten, before they sent them out to the streets to make their money. I couldn't bear to think of Mia in one of those places. I hadn't realized how tightly I was gripping my glass until a strong hand gripped my forearm and stilled my shaking.

"Whoa there, my friend. Are you alright?" La Guerriglia spoke in a low tone so that only I could hear among the crowds of my men gathering in the parlor, preparing for our meeting.

"I'm fine." I scrubbed a hand over my face to try to wipe away the images in my mind.

"You can't go in there thinking like this. You're emotional. Emotions get you killed. Set aside any fears you have, any feelings you have for this girl, and just focus on the mission. It's the only way that you'll survive this and it's the only way you'll have a chance of getting her back."

I nodded, knowing that he was right, but I didn't know how to turn off the turmoil churning inside me. I doubted that I'd be able to gain any control over those feelings until Mia was back in my arms.

Once all the men were gathered, I drew their attention to me. My father sat to one side, watching as I took control of the meeting. Since he had named me as his successor, he'd slowly stepped back, allowing me more responsibility and leadership. While I was grateful for the authority to sanction a mission to save Mia, part of me wished that my father was still the one calling the shots. He had more experience, but I had more passion. That passion would either get me killed or be the driving force to get Mia home.

I gathered with Nic, Alessandro, Enzo, Luca, and Dante to go over our plan before leaving for Tuscany. Each man would have roughly five men who would answer to him, except for La Guerriglia's team of twelve.

"Where's this famous mercenary you told us about?" Dante asked once the meeting was wrapping up.

"His team will be traveling separately. They have their own connections and it's easier to fly under the radar if you keep your groups smaller. Besides, if we have two groups going in separately, we double our chances that one of them will succeed and get Mia out safely."

"And you're sure that he can be trusted? He isn't *family*."

"One hundred percent. I wouldn't risk Mia's life by bringing in someone I didn't trust. He's been loyal to me and my family for years. He takes on other jobs but only if they don't conflict with my family's well-being."

"Good." Dante nodded his approval.

I nodded in return before facing the rest of the men. "Any other questions or concerns before we head out? I want us all to be on the same page."

"I think we're all clear here. We'll have time to brief our men on the ship to make sure that everybody's clear on our mission. Getting Mia out is top priority. And if we have the chance to take out Andrea, we do it," Enzo confirmed.

"All right. Let's do this."

The men filed out of the house, spilling into the yard where their men waited for instructions, but Dario stopped me at the door.

"Are you sure that I can't come along? I care about Mia too."

I slapped my hand on his shoulder and looked at him with a fond expression. Dario was younger than the rest of us, less experienced too. I didn't want to see my younger cousin get hurt. Besides, I had another job for him.

"I know you do. But I'm counting on you to be Papa's right hand while I'm gone. I need you to make sure that you keep Mira out of trouble and help protect Isabella. Andrea's men may be looking for her, so she needs to stay hidden somewhere they won't think to look. I gave her my word and now I need your help in keeping it."

Dario took a deep breath, his shoulders lifting with his newfound determination and purpose. He gave me a sharp nod while meeting my eye.

"You have my word. I will do everything I can to keep her safe and keep Mira out of trouble—as hard as that might be to do." He smirked and I let out a small chuckle before I patted him on the back and climbed into my car.

CHAPTER 6

Mia

Slow breath in.

Blow a long, slow breath out.

Again.

I repeated the words in my mind as I tried to focus on controlling my breathing, instead of on the pain that covered my entire body. For days, I had endured being strung up by my wrists and beaten, left to hang there until I thought my muscles were going to explode then being crammed into the small confines of the dog crate. I had no idea how many days it had been. Time ran together and there was no schedule to my torture. I had no idea if Teo was alive or dead and no way of knowing if anyone would find me.

I was one single person and for all they knew I could be anywhere in the world. It was funny how the world seemed so small with all the technology that we had but yet to really think about one person in all the world really made me feel small and insignificant. The chances of them finding that one person was nearly impossible. I struggled to keep my mind from drifting to darker thoughts. Thoughts of giving in to Andrea's demands. I couldn't do that to my family. I couldn't do that to Teo, but I couldn't stand the torture much longer. He was wearing me down.

My only other option was to hope that Andrea would get tired of dealing with my stubbornness and put me out of my misery. Those were the thoughts that I was most ashamed of. But they were the ones that seemed to creep in more often the longer I was there.

I was pulled from my thoughts by the clinking of keys as someone unlocked the cell door, and I braced myself for what I knew was coming.

Footsteps echoed on the stone floor as they grew near to me, and I tensed, putting up my guard and readying myself for the pain and agony that was to come. The crate door squeaked open, and I held my breath, waiting for the cruel hand to reach inside, grip my hair and yank me out. But it didn't come. For the first time in so many days, it didn't come. The waiting was almost worse.

Andrea's voice came from off in the distance, still within the confines of the cell, but not hovering by the crate door as he usually did. "Come out," he commanded in a gentle yet firm tone that was unlike his usual cruel lit.

I was hesitant but I didn't want to make him angry, so I slowly forced my aching limbs to move until I finally crawled out of the crate. He sat in a chair on the other side of the cell. His posture was rigid and unyielding. "Crawl to me," he said with an authoritative tone.

Although my pride wanted me to scoff at such a demeaning order, I had to pick my battles, and I was too weak to earn any extra cruelty. I crawled slowly, wincing in pain as my muscles screamed from being cramped for so many hours. I barely made it to him before collapsing on the floor.

"You have been through so much these past few days. You need a break." His voice was almost tender which sent alarm bells ringing in my head, though I was too weak to react. "Here, drink."

He put a water bottle to my lips, but I hesitated. Sometimes the water bottles contain water but other times it was alcohol that clouded my mind and made it harder to fight.

"Drink," he commanded in a firmer tone. "You haven't had any water in a day and a half. Your muscles are aching because you're dehydrated."

I tried to lick my dry lips before finally taking the water, but he controlled how much I could drink and only gave me a few sips before pulling it away.

"All this suffering can end. It's not necessary. You can make it all stop," he spoke tenderly as he brushed a strand of hair from my face. "All you have to do is agree to marry me and we can move on. We can get you cleaned up, a nice massage to help ease your muscles, some food perhaps? I know you have to be hungry. You haven't eaten more than a bit of bread in two weeks. You would have fine clothes and gourmet meals with top quality wine, and I would rule both families with you by my side. You are far too lovely to be in a place like this. Will you still deny me? Will you not agree to marry me and make all this suffering stop?"

"Kill me," I rasped in a weak voice that was hardly a whisper.

"What was that?" he said softly, leaning in a little closer to be able to hear me.

"Kill me, please?" I found a little more strength in my voice as I made up my mind.

He wouldn't let me go. His pride would never allow that but maybe I could gain just enough mercy that he would kill me instead. Andrea gently gripped my chin, tilting my face up so that I would look at him.

The corners of his mouth curled up into a sickening sweet smile. "Now what good would you be to me dead? You will be my wife. Maybe this torture is good for you."

"Good for me?" I scoffed, finding a little bit of strength to put behind my voice. "How is this good for me?"

"Because your father sheltered you from the true darkness that comes from the world that we live in. You are arrogant and spoiled. That's why you refused to marry me. That's why you refuse to give in. You think you're better than me." His voice rose along with his anger.

I trembled. I didn't want to seem weak in front of him, but I was.

DEVOTED TO THE ENEMY

"You didn't know how dark this world could get until now. But this is also giving me some time to get to know you. You see, I realize that you are a very selfless, sacrificing woman. You would give up everything, even your life for your family and that only makes me want you as my wife more. It only heightens my determination. But I also realize that I could easily damage you beyond repair before you would ever agree to marry me. It pains me to see such beautiful flesh marred by the stripes of the whip or the ugly bruises on your face."

He ran a crooked finger along my face, dragging his knuckle along my bruised cheek, and I instinctively pulled away. "You should be in fine clothing with your hair and makeup done to perfection. The perfect trophy wife. Your beauty is wasted in a place like this. So, I'm going to do you a favor."

With those words I looked up at him in a combination of something like shock and curiosity.

"Do something for me?" I asked without thinking.

Andrea smiled and nodded. "I'm going to give you a way out. One that will let the suffering stop and give me everything that I want while allowing you not to feel guilty over giving in."

I didn't know what he had planned, but I knew it couldn't be good. Another sense of dread built up in the pit of my stomach.

"Bring her in," Andrea commanded to someone outside of my line of sight and the cell door opened once more with the loud screech before slamming closed again.

A man I hadn't seen before forced another girl into the cell onto her knees beside Andrea, turned to face me. She looked close to my age. Her hair was stringy and unkempt, but she was clean and wearing a slinky cocktail dress that didn't fit with our current situation. I looked at her curiously before looking back at Andrea for an explanation.

"This is Abigail. Abigail is one of my girls." Andrea ran his knuckles down Abigail's cheek, and she flinched at the contact but otherwise didn't respond.

"One of your girls? I asked curiously.

"I own her. Just as I own several other women. A gentleman who owns a club nearby rents her from me to work his *special* VIP rooms."

I looked at her and felt sick for what I knew that she had been through.

"Abigail is a good girl. Aren't you, Abigail?

"Yes sir," she whispered softly, keeping her eyes down.

"You see, Abigail wasn't always such a good girl. She was dumb enough to get knocked up the first year that she was here. By one of those fucking John's of all things. But I was forgiving, wasn't I Abigail?"

"Yes sir," she stated with no emotion.

"Why don't you tell her what I did for you? Let my future wife hear of my benevolence," Andrea urged her.

Abigail looked up at me for a moment before turning her eyes back to the stone floor. "I was allowed to keep the baby. I was allowed to raise her and be her

44

mother. She was cared for and provided for as long as I continued to work at the club and do as I was told without causing any trouble."

"And what happens if you cause trouble?" Andrea coaxed her.

The girl hesitated, her lip trembling, and her eyes glossing over as she looked back up at me with a pitiful expression that I couldn't even put into words. "If I don't do what I'm told, then I will be killed, and my daughter will take my place at the club."

She looked as though she might get sick from just having to speak the words and I couldn't help but gasp.

"How old is your daughter?" I whispered the only question that came to mind.

Abigail swallowed hard around a knot in her throat. I could see the struggle to speak again. Andrea nudged her with his foot.

"Go on. Don't be rude. She asked you a question."

Abigail glanced up at me and took a deep breath. "Eleven."

I looked up at Andrea in surprise and disgust. "She's a child. You wouldn't. You can't."

"On the contrary. Abigail belongs to me so anything that is hers is really mine. Her clothes could be taken away from her in a moment. Her daughter belongs to me. As does her life. Any of these things can be taken in a moment because I own them, and it is my right."

I wanted to throw up. I had no idea things like that actually happened, not in my world, not anywhere close to

45

me. Those were things that you might see in a movie or one of those documentaries, but this was really happening right in front of me, and I didn't know how to wrap my mind around it.

"Why is she here? I asked Andrea. "Why are you telling me this? Why are you showing me this? Do you think this will make me want to marry you more? It makes me sick. It makes me despise you even more than I did before."

"I don't care how it makes you feel. All I care about are results."

"And how is this supposed to help your results?" I spat out my words, finding strength in my disgust.

"That's simple," Andrea said calmly.

He pulled a gun from his side, cocked the hammer back, and pointed it at Abigail's head. She cried out, winced, and began to sob and plead for her life.

"Please? I didn't do anything wrong. I did everything you said. Please? Please don't kill me? Please spare me? I'll do anything.

"You see how a good girl acts? Unfortunately, Abigail, it's not you that has the power to influence the outcome today. It's Mia's. You see my little *topolina*, her life is in your hands. So, make your decision…right here and now.

"Her life and the life of her daughter will be forever changed one way or the other depending on what you say today. Agree to marry me and I will not only spare her life and the life of her daughter, but as a wedding present to you, I will set them both free. Reject me again and I will put a bullet in her head right here and it will be her blood on your hands, and your decision will sentence her daughter to take her place at the club. A childhood ended in one single day. So, what's it going to be?"

"Please don't do this?" I said nervously as I looked between Abigail and Andrea knowing that I couldn't let him kill her. I couldn't let her daughter be condemned to the life that Andrea had in mind. Abigail wailed and cried with sobs that shook her whole body.

"Your decision Mia," Andrea demanded as he pressed the gun into her temple.

"Okay," I cried out and all the fight left me as I resolved to what I had to do. "Okay," I said again, a bit calmer.

"Okay what?" Andrea demanded. He wanted to hear me say the words, but they stuck in my throat.

"Okay what?" He demanded my answer louder as he shook the gun in Abigail's direction.

"Okay. I will marry you." I nearly choked on the words as I forced them out.

CHAPTER 7

Teo

"Alright, the ship's captain wants full deniability, so we are on our own when it comes to boarding. We've been informed that all but two men take a break at the same time of night. That's the best time to sneak on board."

"Luca, do you have eyes on the guy on deck?"

"Yeah. He seems to keep a pretty even pace around the top deck so as long as we time it right, we should be good to go." Luca answered through my earpiece. All the leaders were connected to one system so we could easily stay in communication.

"Enzo, what about you? You see guy number two?"

Enzo snickered. "Yeah. I see him alright. Busy earning his wages by fucking some girl on the other side of the cargo containers."

"So, we should have a good thirty seconds before we have to worry about him," Nic joked, and a couple of the guys chuckled over the line.

"Okay, Luca. As soon as the guy on deck circles back around. Give the order and the first group moves out."

We moved in three groups. One each time the man would pass our location, until all our men were securely on board the cargo ship.

We scattered out, hiding behind large shipping crates, our guns in hand in case anyone discovered us. We may have had the money and manpower to take down the small shipping crew but sometimes stealth outweighed a show of brute strength. We hoped to make it into Corsica undetected to allow for the element of surprise.

When the large packing doors were closed and the ship began to slowly make its way out to sea, we were finally able to let our guards down and relax a bit.

There wouldn't be any reason for the ship's crew to head down to the cargo holding area before the ship docked in Corsica. Even then there would be a small window of time for us to slip out before they made their way to us.

About an hour into our four-hour journey, the door that led into the main part of the ship rattled. We hurried behind boxes and cargo crates with our guns at the ready. We wouldn't be able to risk word getting back to the

Corsicans if anyone spotted us, and I had no desire to leave a trail of bodies along our path. At least not until I found the men I was looking for.

I slipped behind one row of boxes. Keeping out of sight, I slowly worked my way around the cargo containers as the ship worker walked down the main row. Eventually, I passed him so that I could come up behind him if he got too close.

He neared the group of Luca's men, and I held my breath. Any further and Luca would be exposed. I rushed toward him from behind, locking my arms around his neck in a chokehold before he could see them.

The ship worker fought, gripping desperately at my forearms. He tried his best to pry my arms from his throat, but I held tight even as he kicked out, his feet shuffling against the floor. His grip weakened. His motions slowed as the fight left his body just before he went limp. I dragged him out of view of the door and laid him gently on the floor.

"He'll wake up before too long," Enzo warned.

"I know."

"It would be safest if we kill him now quickly and quietly so he can't go back and tell anyone that we're here," Alessandro suggested.

I looked at one of the guys under my command. "Tie him up, blindfold and gag him. Nobody use real names in case he can hear us. We will leave him here for them to find. He won't be able to give any information if he doesn't have any to give."

50

"It's still risky. Wouldn't it be easier just to end him now?" One of the men asked curiously but with no sign of disrespect.

"Easier? In some ways, perhaps. But taking a life should never be easy. And we should never kill just to avoid expending effort. It's lazy, sloppy, and inhumane." My voice was even. I wasn't angry or offended by his question. Most men in my position would have chosen to kill the man but I wanted to do things differently and doing things differently meant being willing to reeducate those under me.

The man nodded thoughtfully before retreating back into the crowd. For the rest of our trip, the majority of the men slept or rested until the ship came to a stop.

"We've docked," I said just loud enough for my men to hear. "Hide until we're sure that they aren't coming down here first."

Once we were sure that the men had climbed off board, one of my contacts at the dock opened the cargo door and we all slipped out under the shadow of night.

He led us around a private area behind several shipping containers where La Guerriglia stood waiting with a dozen of his men and a large eighteen-wheeler at his back.

"I thought you guys could use a ride to the safe house." La Guerriglia kept his voice low.

"We'd appreciate it."

"I figured this would get less attention than chartering a Greyhound." I gave a chuckle, and he slapped my shoulder as he guided me along. "I set up some mattresses in the back. You shouldn't get slammed around too much. You can catch a short nap before we get to the safe house if you want."

"How long of a drive is it?"

"Nearly two hours."

"And how far from there to Andrea's hideout?"

"About half an hour's drive."

"Alright. Thank you, my friend. I'm just ready to get Mia back."

"I've had one of my guys keeping an eye on the compound for some time now and he said he would let us know if anything changes or if they decided to move her."

"Good. Thank you."

I dozed off for a short time on the drive to the safe house, but my mind raced with plans, what ifs, and thoughts of Mia. I just wanted her back and I doubted that I would rest easily until I could finally rest with her in my arms. Even so there was something about traveling that always seemed to make me tired and my eyes drooped heavily. La Guerriglia glanced over at me with a concerned look, but he didn't say a word.

"What is it?" I asked dryly.

"I didn't say anything," he answered, turning his eyes back to the road.

"What you're not saying is *very* loud. You've always been frank with me and it's a trait that I've come to admire so don't stop now. What do you have to say?"

"When was the last time that you slept?"

"I dozed off for about an hour on the ship."

"And before that?" He raised his brow and studied my expression as I thought back.

"Maybe two hours the night before last."

"You can't go on such little sleep. You need to rest."

"I'll rest once Mia is returned to me."

"If you don't rest before then, you could make mistakes. The most dangerous thing on the field is a tired man."

"I just want Mia back safe. I'm not willing to sleep until I know that she's safely back in my arms. God knows what that monster is doing to her."

"And I understand that, but if you want to maximize our chances of getting her back, unharmed, then you need to be at your best. We are already going in outnumbered, outgunned, and with them having the home advantage."

"What do you suggest I do? Sleep cozied up on a soft mattress while Mia's most likely being tortured, held against her will, forced to—"

"You can't think like that. You should be resting so that you can think clearly and get her back safely. Sleeping isn't selfish, Matteo. It's necessary."

"I don't think I can."

"It will be daylight soon after we get to the safe house. I think our best bet is to get some shut eye, make a plan, then strike tomorrow night when we'll have the dark on our side. It will be easier to ambush them."

"You want me to wait an entire day to get Mia back while on the same island as her?"

"I want you to think about this and act smart."

"I trust your battle plans and your military training to help us infiltrate their compound as you did with getting us into their country, but you don't know Mia. Andrea will punish her for escaping before. It's easy for you to say that we should wait. You don't care for her the way I do. I can't bear the thought of her spending one more moment with him."

"Do you know why surgeons don't cut on their own family members? Even if they are the best in their field."

"Because they're too emotionally involved," I answered.

"Exactly. With Mia, you're too emotionally involved to make the right decision. I know you want to get her back, but you don't want her to get caught in the crossfire, do you? You don't want her to end up dead or injured."

"No. I don't want that."

"Good. Then it's settled."

CHAPTER 8

Mia

I couldn't believe the words that had just fallen from my lips. I had agreed to marry Andrea.

"Good." His harsh, angry expression fell away, replaced by a mischievous, evil grin that reminded me of the Grinch. He slipped his gun back into the waistband of his pants and I breathed out a sigh of relief. "I'll have someone summon the priest now. Panic shot through me as the realization sank in. I was going to marry Andrea. I would essentially belong to him, and he was getting the priest. If I didn't do something, say something, it was going to happen that same night.

The idea of being that monster's wife, essentially his property in his mind, to know what he would expect on our wedding night, made me sick but if I had let that little girl lose her mother and take her place I wouldn't have been able to live with myself.

Andrea pulled me up from the floor to stand and started toward the cell door. "Wait," I cried out desperately, not knowing what I was going to say but knowing that I had to come up with something to buy myself a little more time, to hold on to hope for just a little longer.

"What is it?" Andrea looked annoyed.

"Joining two families such as ours," I scrambled for words, trying to think of something that I could say. "It should be a production, don't you agree? Our wedding is a symbol of the joining of our two families and your rise to power. Don't you think that it should be a bit more of a spectacle than a quick little ceremony?"

Andrea looked at me suspiciously, but I could see the wheels in his head turning. "You're right. Sneaking off to get married in the middle of the night is for immature teenagers and scandalous pregnancies."

"I'll have everyone stay up all night preparing and tomorrow evening you will be my bride. For tonight, I'll have you sent to better accommodations so that you can prepare yourself for our wedding. I want you bathed, soaking in a warm tub with scented oils the way they used to in the olden days. I want you pampered so that you look radiant for everyone to see."

"Tomorrow is still a little soon isn't it? I'll need a dress and we need flowers and decorations and to send out invitations."

"I will command everyone to show up. My staff will work through the night to ensure that we have the best of everything. I'll send one of my servants to get you a dress, something more fitting than the modest dress you had planned to wear to marry Teo. My bride's beauty should be on display, not hidden under so many layers of fabric."

"You can do all that in one night?"

"You'd be amazed at all I can accomplish in one night. And you can quit trying to postpone this wedding. You've gained yourself one more night but don't push it."

"Ciro, have *Signora* Monticelli taken to one of our guest rooms. Send in servants to bathe and tend to her. Have anything she would like to eat brought to her room and arrange for a visit from our masseuse as well. I would have her well fed and limbered up for our wedding night."

My stomach dropped at the thought of what he was implying. I felt like breaking down and crying but I knew that I couldn't. I couldn't show any weakness, couldn't let myself feel anything or I would feel everything and that would be more than I could bear. I forced my mind and my emotions to go numb as the guard escorted me from the cell.

My body trembled and my muscles screamed as I was nearly dragged down the hall toward the room that would become my new cell.

I stumbled, weak from the lack of food and minimal water as well as from my tired, beaten body.

I glanced around the home that we were in, it was elegant like something from the past but there were no signs of any exits. I had no idea how I was going to escape. *Even if I do have to marry Andrea, that's not the end. I can still fight. I can still escape once his guard is down. The priests would see fit to annul our marriage once they understood that it was under extreme duress. As long as I was alive and breathing it wasn't over.* I reminded myself.

The guard stopped in front of a large wooden door that was only partially closed. The large deadbolt on the outside gave me a little hope of escaping once I was inside. I struggled against his grasp trying to break free in a desperate attempt to avoid being locked in another, albeit elegant, cage.

Fighting in my state was of no use and he easily shoved me inside the room. "Stupid little, *puttana.*"

I stumbled and tripped, sliding across the tile floor as my body hit the ground.

"Someone will be in soon to bathe you." And with that he slammed the door shut. There was a loud clank as the lock slipped into place.

I didn't even have the energy to pull myself off the floor. I laid there in the silence, racking my brain for an idea, some way of getting out of the mess I was in. I had barely slept in days or weeks. I didn't know, and I wasn't even sure that I was thinking clearly.

It wasn't long before the clanking sound of the lock drew my attention and I sat up, scrambling away from the door toward the foot of the bed. When the door opened, an older French lady walked inside.

She was dressed in a maid's uniform and her hair was pulled into a tidy bun. "*Bonjour, mademoiselle.* I'm here to assist you in your bath."

I suddenly felt shy, remembering my nakedness, and I struggled to wrap my arms around myself enough to shield my body from her view. "I don't need help bathing. I can do it myself."

"*Oui,* I'm sure you can *mademoiselle,* but *Monsieur* Romano insists upon it. He gave very strict, detailed instructions. Now let's not dilly dally. Up you go."

She struggled to help me off the floor while carrying a large tote bag that I hadn't noticed until then and led me to the en suite bathroom.

She helped me to sit on the edge of the bathtub while she ran the water and poured fragrant oils into the warm bath. Once the tub was filled she helped to lower me into the warm water that caressed my aching muscles and joints. She topped off the water with a few scattered rose petals before hurriedly grabbing a sponge and dunking it into the water, scrubbing my arms, shoulders, and back. As she began to work her way over to my chest, I grabbed her arm gently.

"I can do the rest. Thank you." I took the sponge from her and began bathing myself while she busied herself washing my hair.

When she was done she took the sponge from me and packed up her bag again. I will let you have a little time to soak, it should help ease your sore muscles. And while you soak I'll make sure that someone is bringing your dinner.

"*Grazie,*" I said sincerely.

Once she left, I leaned my head back and closed

my eyes, trying to forget where I was for just a moment. I pictured Teo, searching, unable to find me. *And what if he finds me after the wedding? Would he see me as ruined?* I was no virgin but the idea of me being with someone like Andrea Romano made me shutter. If I married him—if we went through with the wedding night, nothing would ever be the same. I would be ruined, if not in Teo's eyes, in my own.

Maybe it was exhaustion or my body's way of giving in, but I soon dozed off to sleep. A few minutes later, I woke with a start as I slipped under the water and jolted upright, choking and gasping for air.

Then the thought crossed my mind. *It would be so easy for me to slip under the water and just let go. There would be no more beatings, no more restraints, no more Andrea. I would be free from this horrible existence that he was forcing me into.*

I closed my eyes and took a shaky breath as tears silently streamed down my cheeks. It would be so easy. I blew out my breath slowly and let myself slip beneath the surface of the water.

Within just a few moments my lungs began to scream for air, burning and aching and I popped up out of the water, sucking in a desperate rush of air. I quickly unplugged the drain as if it was the water's fault. I couldn't believe what I had considered.

I couldn't do it. I couldn't bring myself to end my life no matter how miserable the circumstances seemed. Death was too final. As long as I was alive, there was hope.

CHAPTER 9

Mia

The thought of what I'd almost done lingered in my mind the rest of the night and even though I was starving from the miniscule amount of food Andrea had given me for the past couple of weeks, I was hardly able to do more than pick on my food. I reminded myself that I needed to keep up my strength for whatever was to come, and by the end of the night, I had managed to clear my plate.

I needed a plan, a way to escape but more than that, I needed hope. I still had no way of knowing whether or not Teo was alive. At the very least, I had my own family I was certain would eventually come looking for me. That didn't mean that they would arrive before I had to marry Andrea. I had to come to terms with the fact that there was a very real possibility that I would have to marry him and even worse share a night with him.

The thought of being intimate with him disgusted me. The only way I was going to get through it was to put up emotional walls like I'd never done before. I had to quit feeling anything and focus on surviving. Unfortunately, I had no idea how I was going to do that.

With all the horrible things that I knew was coming the next day, I feared that I would spend my entire night tossing and turning with nightmares or be unable to fall asleep at all, but my body had been worn out. Between the torture, lack of food and sleep, being locked up in that tiny kennel or stretched out with the shackles as I dangled from the ceiling, my body welcomed a dreamless sleep.

"*Signora* Monticelli? Breakfast." The young woman's voice stirred me from my sleep, and I sat up with a jolt, looking around to realize where I was.

I looked at her with confusion as I rub the sleep from my eyes. "I'm sorry. What?"

"*Signore* Romano sent me up with breakfast and coffee. He requests that you are well fed and pampered today while he is busy making the final wedding arrangements."

I sat up and she placed the tray of food over my lap. "Thank you. Did he say what time the wedding is taking place tonight?" I tried to keep my voice casual, but the woman cast me a worried glance anyway.

"Seven-thirty." She kept busy and avoided meeting my eye as she poured coffee into my cup.

"Thank you. For breakfast and the information." I spoke kindly to her because if her body language was any indication, she was not supportive of Romano's plans. She seemed just as trapped there as I was.

"You're welcome, *Signora* Monticelli."

"Call me Mia, please. Can I ask your name?"

She looked a bit uncomfortable as she glanced up at me before turning her eyes back down toward the floor. "Elena."

"It's nice to meet you Elena, even though the circumstances might not be ideal." I smiled sheepishly at her, hoping that she would see that I wasn't a threat. "How long have you worked for *Signore* Romano?"

"Two years." She looked uncomfortable at my questions, but I found myself pulled toward her and wanted to know more.

"Is he a good boss to work for?"

Her eyes widened and her words rushed out. "Oh, yes. He is a wonderful boss. I would not wish to work for anyone else. He is fair and kind to his employees." Her words sounded scripted.

"I see. That's very fortunate for you then I guess. How did you come to start working for him?"

"Excuse me, *Signora*, but I should get back downstairs to help with preparations for the wedding this evening."

"Of course. I wouldn't want to get you in any trouble." I was disappointed that I wasn't able to get any more information from her, but I suspected that she had most likely been taken and was not just an employee in Andrea's home.

Elena scurried out like a scared little mouse that had been exposed from the shadows for too long.

Being alone again brought my thoughts back to the wedding and what would be happening after. I had to do whatever it took to save my life and I had to find a way to be okay with that.

I ate my breakfast and drank my coffee as I stared out the third story window with no means of escape. The night before, I had opened my window and tried tugging at the ornate iron bars, but they were strong and unyielding.

Time dragged on with nothing to do. I looked around, trying to find something to help aid in my escape or even just to pass the time, but the room was completely void from anything other than a couple of changes of clothing and some toiletries.

I hated the thought of the wedding and knew that time was running out for me to get away but there was also nothing I could do in a locked room. Time seemed to move too slowly and too fast all at once.

Before I knew it, the older maid from the night before came into my room to help me prepare myself for the wedding. I moved through the motions, but I was numb, only doing what was asked of me without feelings or emotion.

She excused herself for a moment and came back with a long garment bag that she draped over the bed. "Shall I open this for you?"

"No. I'll get dressed on my own. Thank you."

I waited until she left the room before slowly approaching the bag like it was a snake ready to strike. It might as well have been, because once I put it on, my life would be over.

I held my breath. *You're doing what you have to do to survive and to ensure that no innocents drown in the wake.*

I blew out my breath and unzipped the bag. I was surprised by the choice of dress Andrea had selected for me. It was not what I would have expected from him at all. Extremely traditional with an A-line hem, lots of lace, and tulle. It wasn't what I would have picked out for myself but after the monstrosity that Gio had given me, I could honestly say that it wasn't the ugliest wedding dress I'd ever owned.

I slipped off my robe and stepped into the dress, pulling it over my hips and shoulders. I had to work on the zipper to get it up on my own, but it was better than having someone else do it and I was grateful for the moment alone.

I looked in the mirror and started to sob uncontrollably, cupping my hands over my face, and sliding down to the floor.

I don't want this. This isn't how things were supposed to turn out.

There was a firm knock on the bedroom door that made me jump.

"*Signore* Romano has sent me to retrieve you. He says that it is time." I realized the voice as Pietro and tensed.

I pulled myself off of the floor and swiped the last remaining tears from my face.

"You can do this. You *have* to do this," I whispered to myself.

"Signora," Pietro snapped impatiently.

"I'm coming." I opened the door with a jerk and looked up at the burly man who looked utterly ridiculous in his ill-fitting tux. "Let's get this over with."

"*Signore* Romano ordered that I give you his gift before escorting you down. He wants you to wear it for the ceremony." He held out a small, elongated box for me to open.

I lifted the lid of the box and pulled out the inch wide diamond necklace.

"It's a choker." I pulled it out of the box and examined the obviously expensive piece of jewelry completely covered in small diamonds. I ran my fingers along the length and froze at the little padlock attached to the clasp. "It's a glorified collar."

"*Signore* Romano wants there to be no mistaking who you belong to."

"I will not wear this. I may be marrying him, but I belong to no one. This is insulting." I tossed the diamond strand to the floor and stormed down the hall.

"*Signore* isn't going to be happy that you aren't wearing his gift."

"Then I guess he won't be happy. Frankly, I don't care "

"You will."

I turned around at the bottom of the stairs to look

back at him. "What's that supposed to mean?"

"You will quickly learn that your life will be much easier if you can make *Signore* happy. He's much harder to get along with when you aren't agreeable."

The music struck up, interrupting my retort and Pietro continued. "It's time."

My entire body began to shake as two guards opened the French doors that lead to the courtyard.

I can't do this. I can't.

My stomach twisted into knots and my knees buckled but Pietro grabbed hold of my arm before I could fall and forced me forward.

He walked me down the aisle where only a couple dozen people stood watching. I was still shaking when I reached Andrea and Pietro passed me over to him.

Andrea forced a smile and pulled me into a hug. "You're not wearing my gift," he ground out through clenched teeth.

"I may be becoming your wife, but I am nobody's slave." I hissed in his ear, and he forced a smile for his guests as he pulled away.

"You will pay for your disobedience tonight," he whispered, and a sick feeling gripped my stomach and twisted.

"Dearly beloved, we are gathered here today to join this man and this woman in holy matrimony..." the priest continued but my mind began reeling as another wave of panic set in. I couldn't breathe and my whole world began to spin.

Andrea squeezed my hand so hard it hurt, and I realized that everyone was waiting for me to say something.

"I'm sorry what?"

"Please repeat after me," the priest repeated. "I, Maria Monticelli, take Andrea Romano to be my lawfully wedded husband..."

I reluctantly repeated the words.

"To cherish, honor, and obey..."

I glanced curiously at Andrea, and he grinned a wicked grin. "I thought you would appreciate me removing love from your requirements."

I ground my teeth together, hesitating for a moment before opening my mouth to force the bitter words from my lips, but just before any sound was able to come out, I was interrupted by a loud crash as back doors violently burst open.

CHAPTER 10

Mia

There was an explosion of gunfire from intruding men who flowed out of the house with what I could only describe as military precision as they flooded into the courtyard. Surprised by the sudden invasion, Andrea's men were slower to react, pulling their guns and beginning to shoot only after half a dozen of their men had dropped.

I scanned my surroundings for a place to run, bolting toward a patch of ornamental trees to the far right of the yard before Andrea had a chance to stop me.

Bullets exploded as they hit dirt and trees all around us, a few causing their intended targets to stumble backward before falling to the ground.

I had no sympathy for Andrea and the evil men who worked for him, but I didn't trust the mystery intruders either.

I was almost to the trees when I came face to face with one of the attacking men. I gasped and flinched in anticipation for what he might do but instead of aiming his gun at me, he paused long enough for me to run past him before continuing on his way.

Whoever the men were, it wasn't their plan to hurt me.

I hurried behind a cluster of trees and ducked down, not risking peeking out to keep an eye on the fighting. It wasn't long before one of Andrea's men caught me by the arm from behind.

"There you are. *Signore* Romano will want to make sure you don't slip away in the chaos. Come on."

He tugged my arm hard, causing me to lose my footing and I stumbled, breaking his grip on me as my knee hit the hard dirt.

There was a loud blast. Closer than before and Andrea's man fell to the ground with an already growing bloodstain near the center of his chest.

I screamed and ducked but no bullet came for me. The man wasn't moving, and the shooter moved on, so I ran over to Andrea's man's body and grabbed his discarded gun mere feet from where he'd fallen.

Maybe this is my chance, the answer to my prayers.

I couldn't let the opportunity pass. I glanced around the yard that had erupted into an all-out war zone. No one seemed to be paying much attention to me. I held the gun tight and darted for the large iron gate that led outside of the courtyard and hopefully to somewhere I could escape from.

One of Andrea's men stopped in my way, and I froze.

"Move," I commanded.

"If I let you get away, I'm as good as dead." He reached for me and without thinking of anything but that moment, I pulled the trigger.

The man flew back and stumbled into a flower bed, but I couldn't take the time to think of what I'd done, I had to keep going.

I reached the gate, but the thick metal chain and padlock secured it in place. I sat the gun down in the grass in order to use both hands and pulled with every ounce of my strength but before I knew it, Andrea came from behind me and gripped my upper arm with bruising force.

"Not so fast. You weren't thinking of leaving without me, were you, my dear wife?"

"We never..."

He fumbled with his keys to unlock the chain. The sound of shooting grew closer as he struggled to keep a hold on me. Just as he unlocked the gate, I yanked my arm out of his grasp, rounding to elbow him right in the nose and he stumbled back. I tried to run but he grabbed a fist full of my hair and pulled me back. I stumbled against him, his forearm across my throat, pinning me to him as he forced me through the gate. Andrea froze on the other side as we came face to face with Nic and Alessandro along with some other men behind them.

Andrea pulled us back, but Luca and Enzo came up behind us. I cried out as Andrea tightened his grip on me, using me as a human shield. He pulled his gun from his back and held it up to my temple just as another group of men came to join Nic and Alessandro's group.

"Teo?" I gasped, my heart swelling with overflowing joy at seeing him alive and in one piece.

Teo's eyes widened, and he froze when his gaze landed on the gun pointed at me.

"Nobody come any closer or I shoot her."

"It's over, Andrea. You're surrounded. There's no way you're getting out of here with her," Teo barked.

Even considering the situation I was in, a wave of relief washed over me just knowing that Teo and his men were there.

"As long as I have her it's not over. It's never over." Andrea's voice lifted.

"And if you shoot her then you won't have her anymore," Alessandro reminded him.

"I think Teo would be more heartbroken than I." Andrea pressed the gun harder against my temple and I tensed.

He was right. Andrea had more leverage because he didn't care, not really. I met Teo's gaze, hoping that he would be able to see what I couldn't say. I widened my eyes for a moment and gave the slightest hint of a nod.

Teo glanced at Andrea and back to me, worry and uncertainty etching creases in his brow. I was worried too but we had to do something.

72

"What's it going to be, Teo? Are you going to get out of my way and let me go or are you going to watch as I shoot the pretty donna in the head?"

Teo met my eye again and I nodded with more determination in my expression and his worry eased as determination took over.

I let my head bob slightly with each number as I counted in my head.

One...Two...Three...

With the last nod, I let out a nervous breath before twisting and throwing my elbow back as hard as I could into Andrea's midsection. His grip loosened as soon as my elbow struck, and I ducked.

A loud crack rattled my ears. I glanced in the direction of the noise, seeing Teo with his gun still extended before turning my attention to Andrea who lay motionless on the ground.

"Mia," Teo cried out, drawing my attention.

I ran, and he opened his arms as I crashed into him. I threw my arms around him, engulfed in his strong embrace.

Teo kissed my temple, as his hands practically crushed me to his chest. "I thought I'd lost you," Teo murmured softly into my hair.

"They told me that you were dead." I wrapped my arms tighter around him, never wanting to let go.

"Turns out, I'm not that easy to kill."

"Teo, we need to move unless you really want to

test that theory," Alessandro tugged Teo back the way they came and me along with them.

We ran toward a small side gate, but my legs were shaky and weak from my time in the cell. I stumbled, but Teo's grip lifted me back to my feet.

A few of Andrea's men tried to follow us but Teo and our group shot each one without hesitation and we pushed on.

We made it to a black sports car with only two seats and I looked at them puzzled.

"This is our getaway car. The others will go back and finish this."

"We're just going to leave your friends behind?" I asked in astonishment.

"We are friends, we are also family, his captains, and his soldiers when needed. As we will be yours once you become donna to the Venturi family." Alessandro's words touched me, and I reached out to gently grasp his arm.

"Be careful. And thank you."

"You're welcome." I released his arm and Alessandro looked at Teo. "Get her out of here. We've got this. We'll meet up as planned."

"Thank you, my friend." Teo and Alessandro clasped arms before we climbed in the car and the other men returned to the fight.

Teo started the car and it roared to life while I quickly buckled my seat belt.

"I feel bad leaving them behind."

"I know. But our first priority is getting you to safety. They are trained for this sort of thing."

I silently nodded, still feeling like I should have stayed to fight but ultimately knowing that I'd be no good to anyone in my current state.

Teo sped out of our hiding spot and once we hit the paved road, he laid on the gas, sending me jolting back against my seat. I gasped and Teo gently took my hand.

"It's okay. I've got you."

CHAPTER 11

Teo

We sped down the road for over half an hour before pulling off onto a series of smaller windy roads that led to the safe house where I'd arranged for us to stay. It was an elegant mansion, perched on the side of a cliff that overlooked the ocean below.

I stopped the car right in front of the door and rounded the car to open Mia's door for her.

"What is this place?" Mia gazed up at the beautiful beach house with a hint of wonder in her voice.

I offered Mia my hand and helped her out of the car. "It's my associate's vacation home. He said that I was always welcome to use it if I was ever in Corsica."

"That was generous of him."

I smiled, placing my hand on the small of her back to lead her into the house. "He owed me. Come on. Let's get inside. I'm sure you could use some food. Maybe a warm bath."

We just made it to the top of the front steps when Mia stopped me. "What about the other men?"

"They won't have to be as careful now that you aren't there. I told them to wipe out everyone."

"Everyone?" Mia tensed, a panicked look washing over her face. "Teo. They can't. There's a girl there, Abigail. She's being held against her will. They force her to...*do* things. And a housekeeper, Elena. I'm pretty sure she wasn't there of her own choosing."

"Give me a description. I'll call my men and get them to be on the lookout for them."

"Abigail has a daughter, too. I've never seen her but she's eleven. Andrea was allowing her to keep her daughter as long as she did what he said, but he threatened awful things if she doesn't." Mia trembled and I wrapped my arm around her to pull her closer to me.

"Okay, I'll let Nic know all that."

I pulled out my phone and dialed Nic's number but there was no answer, so I hung up and dialed Alessandro who answered on the second ring.

"Hey, boss. We're just wrapping things up here."

"You do as I instructed?"

"All the men are either dead or rounded up for questioning. Women are safely restrained until we can sort out who they are and what they are doing here."

"Good. I'm looking for two particular women and a young girl."

"Does Mia know? Somehow she doesn't seem like the sharing kind," he teased, and I couldn't help but smile as I shook my head at him.

"One's name is Elena, a housekeeper who was there against her will. Another sounds like one of Andrea's *special* girls. Her name is Abigail. Mia's going to give you a description." I put the phone on speaker and looked at Mia expectantly.

"Okay, I'm heading to where we're holding the women now. Go ahead, Mia."

"She's about my age. Straight hair, big brown eyes, a little on the thin side. I don't think Andrea fed her very well."

"And you said her name is Abigail?"

"Yes."

Alessandro's voice faded as he directed his words at the people on his end, but we could still make out what he was saying. "Alright, listen up. I'm looking for a girl named Abigail. Where's Abigail?"

There was some nondescript talking on the other end before Alessandro's voice came back on the line. "No one is fessing up. But I think I found who you're looking for. She fits the description and looked nervous when I called out her name. I just texted over a picture. Tell me if that's her."

I checked my phone and pulled up the image before holding it up to Mia. "That her?"

"Yes, that's Abigail. Oh, thank God. She's okay. What about her daughter?"

Again, Alessandro's voice lowered, and we had to strain to hear him. "I know you're Abigail. Why are you not being honest with me? I also know that you have a daughter that I'm sure you're eager to get back to."

"Her daughter is eleven," Mia called out over the line and Alessandro changed his questions accordingly.

"I know she's eleven. Probably missing her mama about now. Where is she?"

"I'll never tell you anything," Abigail said sternly.

"Let me talk to her," Mia demanded, and I was shocked by the strength in her voice.

"Okay. Here she is."

"Abigail? It's Mia. From the cell yesterday. It's okay to tell those men where your daughter is. You can trust them."

"No. It's a trick. They are making you say that to get her."

"No, Abigail. Please, this isn't a trick. I want to make sure that you and your daughter are safe."

"I don't believe you. If they aren't forcing you, then come in here and see me yourself."

Mia glanced at me, and I shook my head while mouthing '*no way.*' But Mia lifted her brow and tilted her head to the side as if challenging me. I shook my head again and covered the phone receiver. "It's not safe."

"Alessandro said that they had everyone secured."

"Yes, but—"

"Teo, this girl has been through hell. She has no reason to trust you or Alessandro, but she has a reason to trust me."

"Why would she trust you?"

Mia flinched for a split second. If I had blinked, I would have missed it, but it was there. "Because I agreed to marry Andrea to save her, and her daughter's lives."

"You what?" It was like a sucker punch to the gut.

"I agreed to go through with the wedding so that he wouldn't kill her and start pimping out her daughter like he does her."

"What a bastard. I'm so glad he's finally dead," I muttered to myself. "I still don't want you going back there."

"Seeing me there, *free*, is the only way that she's going to feel safe enough to maybe tell us where her daughter is so that we can help them both."

"No, Mia. I'm not going to let you go back there. It's not worth risking your safety. Andrea could still have backup coming."

"Teo, I thought things had changed. I thought that we were past this."

I let out a resigned sigh. "Fine. But we won't stay long. Just long enough to find her daughter and we're back out.

"Deal." I uncovered the phone's mic to let Mia respond. "Okay, Abigail. We're on our way back."

"Back? From where?"

"A safe place nearby but we're on our way."

"Oh...okay."

"I'll see you soon. And Abigail, everything's going to be okay."

"I hope you're right." The girl, Abigail, had a hint of hope in her voice as they hung up.

I could understand Mia's desire to help the woman and her daughter. They were in a rough situation and Mia had a good heart. I just hoped that it didn't put her in danger.

I escorted Mia back to the car and helped her in before rounding to the driver's side. Her captivity had done a number on her. She didn't walk with as much confidence as she had before. She was quieter and when she slipped into the seat of my car, I noticed a wince.

Seeing Mia in pain made me want to bring that bastard, Andrea, back to life just so that I could kill him in a more painful, time-consuming way. A quick shot to the chest was far too easy for a sadistic monster like him.

I drove down the road, wishing that we were heading out of Corsica and not back to Andrea's. Even with the place under the control of my men, I didn't trust that the Romanos didn't have something else up their sleeve. I had learned before never to stand in Mia's way when she got that determined look in her eye, but that didn't mean I wasn't going to do everything that I could to make sure that she was in and out of there quickly and safely.

Instead of pulling up on the side of the house like I had before, I pulled up to the front, not worried about hiding the car. Luca and some of his men waited out front.

"Hey boss, Alessandro said that you two were coming back. Something about a girl?" Luca asked as I helped Mia from the car.

"Yeah, just gotta handle some business really fast then I'm getting Mia out of this place for good."

"Well, he's got the girl waiting for you in the living room, right off the entryway."

"Good, thank you." I placed my hand on the small of Mia's back and began leading her up the steps when my phone chimed with an incoming message.

+39 06 373 8001: I need to see you. It's urgent.

I didn't recognize the number, but I hesitated at the bottom of the stairs to reply.

Matteo: Who is this?

+39 06 373 8001: Anna. Please, meet me. We need to talk. In person.

Mia stopped at the top of the stairs and looked back at me with a mix of curiosity and concern. "Everything okay?"

I sent a quick, one-handed text back without looking at my phone.

Matteo: I think you have the wrong number.

I set my phone to vibrate as I slipped it into my pocket. The text was strange, but I had to put that out of my mind and focus on getting Mia in and out of that house and that God forsaken island as soon as possible.

I forced a smile and hurried up the steps. "Everything's good."

My phone buzzed with another incoming message that I ignored. I ushered Mia into the house where two of Alessandro's men stood in the entryway.

"Where's Alessandro?"

"In there. With the girl." One of the men standing guard pointed me in the direction of the living room.

"Thanks. Come on. The sooner we get this taken care of, the sooner we can get you out of here and to somewhere safe." I hurried Mia into the living room where Alessandro and the girl I assumed was Abigail sat across from each other on stuffy old chairs that looked like whoever had bought them was trying way too hard to be prestigious.

Abigail stood up excitedly when she spotted Mia.

"You really came."

"Of course, I did." Mia hurried over to Abigail. "I'm so glad that you are safe. I was worried about you with all the fighting."

"I wouldn't say that I'm exactly safe. I'm surrounded by a bunch of strange men with guns." Abigail gave me a distrusting glance, but Mia got her attention back on her.

"But you trust me, right?"

"*Sì.* You sacrificed yourself for my daughter and me."

"Good. Then trust me when I say that you can trust Teo and his men."

"How do you know?"

"Teo is my fiancé. He came here to rescue me from Andrea. He *killed* Andrea."

Abigail's eyes widened as she looked up at me in surprise. "This is true? You killed *Signore* Romano?"

"I did. And my men have either captured or killed all his men on the property. You are safe now," I assured her.

Abigail slowly shook her head, looking less elated than I would have expected from finding out that her tormentor was dead. "Andrea was just the tip of the iceberg. He has a lot of connections in Corsica and Italy. None of us are safe."

"I'll admit I don't have as many connections as I'd like in Corsica but in Italy? I have the power, or Mia and my family do."

"You?" Abigail looked at Mia doubtfully, but Mia nodded.

"I am donna of the Monticelli family, and this is Matteo Venturi, future don to the Venturi family."

"If that's true, then we need to get out of Corsica and back into your territory quickly." Abigail looked nervous.

"Why? What do you know?"

"One night when I was...entertaining *Signore* Romano, I overheard him on the phone. He was talking to some Corsican don about helping him take you down. He has more people on his side here than he does in Italy "

"Then let us help you. We can get your daughter and bring both of you with us back to Italy."

Abigail hesitated, looking from me to Mia before nodding. "Okay, but I go to get my daughter with Mia. No one else."

"Like hell—" I started but Mia interrupted.

"Teo."

"You aren't going somewhere with some woman you barely know when we are in enemy territory. It's not happening. I let you come back to talk to her, but this is where I draw the line."

"Okay, what if the men stay out of sight? Just in case we get into trouble."

Abigail nodded hesitantly, finally giving in. "Okay. Maria is being kept in a small cottage not far from here. An older widow takes care of her but she's afraid of Andrea too so she will only help if I can convince her that he's really dead."

I turned to Alessandro. "Have one of the men text me a photo of Andrea's body. That should be enough to get the widow to trust us. Then have everyone clear out and get to the safe houses. I don't trust that the Corsicans won't come looking for us here."

"You got it."

"I'm going to take Luca with me. Get the rest of the men out as soon as possible." I turned from Alessandro to Mia. "Let's go. We don't have time to waste."

CHAPTER 12

Teo

We pulled up to a small cottage out of the way. The house was in good shape, but the yard hadn't been tended to in a while. For Abigail and her daughter to have such a set routine that her daughter had a caretaker in Corsica, meant that Andrea had more of a hold there than I had originally thought. That knowledge made me want to get Mia out of there even faster. Nothing seemed to be what I thought it was and even though Andrea was dead he still had his father and two brothers that I would eventually have to deal with.

Killing the heir to the Romano crime family would not be without consequence and knowing that they had the Corsicans on their side meant that it was going to be more of a challenge than I had originally anticipated. All I wanted was to find Abigail's daughter and get Mia out of Corsica and back to our city as quickly as possible. There, at least I had more control.

I climbed out of the driver's seat and Luca out of the back, and we both rounded the car to open the girls' doors. We had taken one of the SUVs since the sports car had no room for the extra passengers.

Abigail eagerly headed toward the door, but I grabbed Mia's hand and pulled her back gently for a moment.

"Be careful. If anything looks off, or even feels off, trust your instincts and get out of there. I don't like that you're going in without me and I wish you would reconsider."

"I'll be fine. We will all be fine. We just need to get Maria and get out of here."

"Okay. I'm trusting you on this."

"Thank you."

"For what?"

"For treating me like a partner, like we're a team."

I gently cupped her cheek in the palm of my hand and brought my forehead to hers. "Just don't make me regret it." I smiled softly and pressed a gentle kiss to her lips.

"Don't worry." Mia smiled. "I wouldn't want to have to hear you say that you told me so." She smirked playfully and I couldn't help but let out a soft chuckle.

"Mia," Abigail whispered loud enough that we could hear her, and she motioned for Mia to join her by the door.

Mia hurried over to Abigail while Luca and I took our places in the car.

I watched Mia like a hawk, ignoring the vibration of new messages coming in on my phone. Abigail knocked. It didn't take long for a woman to answer the door. She looked concerned to see Abigail standing there. Her stance became guarded as I studied her body language while they talked. Abigail showed the woman her phone and after a few minutes of Abigail talking, the woman hesitantly let them inside. I was nervous about having Mia somewhere where I couldn't even see what was going on but there was nothing I could do but trust in her judgment. I had to learn to trust her if our relationship was ever going to work. She was too strong-willed to just go along with whatever I said to do. She would not be some princess, protected and locked in a tower. I had learned that the hard way.

I had to distract myself for a moment or I was going to go crazy, jump up and ransack the house to drag Mia back out so I pulled out my phone to check on the messages that had been flowing in periodically for the past hour.

+39 06 373 8001: Is this or is this not Matteo Venturi?

+39 06 373 8001: Please. I need to talk to you. It's extremely important.

+39 06 373 8001: You really don't remember me?

+39 06 373 8001: I thought you were different from your brother. I guess I was wrong.

+39 06 373 8001: Please meet with me? I need to speak with you.

That girl really wasn't giving up. My anxiety over the situation with Mia transformed into irritation at the string of ill-timed texts so I quickly responded.

Matteo: You have something to say, then say it.

+39 06 373 8001: Not through texts. This needs to be face to face.

Matteo: Not a good time.

+39 06 373 8001: do you really think that I would be blowing up your phone if it wasn't important?

Matteo: I don't know. I don't know you.

+39 06 373 8001: Oh yes you do. (Image attached)

I clicked on the attached image and my whole body tensed as I gripped the phone tighter. There on my phone, was a photo of me and a pretty blonde in a tight cocktail dress, my hand obscenely high on her bare thigh as she practically straddled me. I had no recollection of her or that night.

I zoomed in closer to the background. We were at one of our family-owned clubs and Gio was there with a girl on either side.

I remembered that night, going out with Gio. He had just found out that he was arranged to be married to the heir to the Monticelli family and that their don had just died.

The idea of being tied down forever to one woman was not what Gio had been wanting but he knew that it was what he needed to gain more power, so he said that he wanted to go out celebrating and blow off some steam at the same time. He invited me to go along. Even though I had originally declined his offer, my father thought it would be a good idea for me to go and keep an eye on Gio to make sure that he didn't go too far as he often did when we had so much riding on their marriage.

I remembered going to the club and ordering a drink. Two was my usual limit when I was going out with Gio. One of us had to keep our wits and it was always me. But the rest of that night was a blur. I remembered waking up the next morning wondering how I had gotten so drunk. I have been disappointed in myself for letting my guard down and letting myself get out of hand. Gio had been so smug about the fact that I had lost control that night, but I was always suspicious that he had slipped something into my drink. I had just never had the proof or a reason to pursue answers. It was done. It was over. And there had been no real harm.

Was the girl in the image really Anna? And if it was really her, what was so important that she needed to talk to me about three months later? Had she seen that Mia and I were going to get married and decided to what? Blackmail me with the photos? It was before Mia, and I ever got together so there was nothing for me to be blackmailed with.

Matteo: I'm going to assume that the girl in the picture is you?

+39 06 373 8001: Wow, you really don't remember me at all, do you?

Matteo: The whole night was a bit of a blur.

+39 06 373 8001: more of a reason that we need to talk in person.

Matteo: Out of town on business. I won't be able to meet until next week at the earliest.

I had to admit that the image made me curious especially considering how persistent the girl was being. But I had more important things to think about at that moment like the fact that Mia was still not out of that house.

+39 06 373 8001: Name a place. A city, a country. I'll come to you.

Matteo: That desperate to meet with me?

I wrote the last text as more of a snide remark than a serious question, but her answer made me sit up straighter in my seat and an uneasy feeling settled in my chest.

+39 06 373 8001: Yes.

Motion from outside the car caught my attention and I looked up to see Mia, Abigail, and a young girl I assumed was Maria walked out of the house with a couple of full garbage bags in Abigail's hands.

I put my phone away and climbed out of the car to meet Mia and the girls on their way out.

"This must be Maria." I smiled at the young girl, but her eyes widened in fear. She grabbed ahold of Abigail's arm and tucked herself behind her mother.

"No, mama. Please? I don't want to go with him." The poor girl's voice cracked, and she started to sob.

"It's okay, *cocca*. Like I told you, Mia and her friends are going to help us go far away from this place. Somewhere we can be happy and safe."

"You promise?"

"I promise."

"Can I take those for you?" I nodded my head toward the two trash bags and Abigail smiled gratefully, offering them to me.

"Thank you. We didn't exactly have suitcases to pack her things in."

"These work just as well." I smiled and walked the trash bags around to the trunk of the SUV. "Mia," I called out to her as the three of them approached the vehicle. Can I talk to you for a minute?

"Sure. Is something wrong?"

"That girl is clearly terrified of men. And I don't blame her considering that the main one she probably had interaction with was Andrea, but I was thinking it probably wouldn't be best for her and Abigail to be in the back seat with Luca. Would you mind switching with him so that she'll feel more comfortable?"

"Of course. How considerate of you. Thank you for noticing that. It didn't seem like she had it bad in the cottage, but I can't imagine living with that type of constant fear."

Mia gently squeezed my arm before leaning in to press her lips gently to mine.

"I'm so glad that you're okay. Relatively, at least. We still need to sit down and talk about everything that happened while you were with Andrea." Mia looked uncomfortable and I gently tucked a stray strand of hair behind her ear. "This time with him was different, wasn't it? It took more of a toll on you. I can see it."

"I don't want to talk about this. Not now."

"Okay." I took a step back to give her space. "But soon."

"Soon." She gave me a weak smile. "Let's get out of here."

"Good idea."

CHAPTER 13

Mia

We arrived back at the safe house with Abigail and Maria. As we walked into the elegant mansion, I let out a small sigh of relief. We weren't out of danger yet, but I felt better being somewhere that Teo and his men controlled.

"Abigail, Maria, you both must be hungry. I had some of my men stock the kitchen to hold us over until we leave. Please, go help yourself," Teo said in his usual charming voice and the two of them hurried off to the kitchen.

"How about you, can I get you something?" Teo gently tucked a strand of my hair behind my ear and softly pressed his lips to mine.

"More of that would be nice." I smiled.

"Soon," Teo promised. "I want you to have time to heal and build your strength back up first."

I nodded but he leaned in to kiss me once more.

"You said until we leave. When are we leaving?"

"As soon as possible. But we still have to figure out how we were going to get an extra two people out of Corsica undetected."

"I'm sorry for putting a kink in your plans."

"You know I don't mind a little kink." Teo smirked playfully and I slapped his arm, feigning disapproval which made him laugh.

"In all seriousness though, thank you for helping Abigail and her daughter and for trusting me enough to let me do it my way."

"Oh, I learned my lesson about going up against you last time." Teo smiled affectionately. "I'm just glad that you're okay. When I found out that Gabe had taken you, I was thrown. But then to find out that Andrea had gotten you again. I knew he wouldn't make the same mistakes as last time. I was worried that we wouldn't be able to find you."

"How *did* you find me?"

"Gianni's wife, of all people."

"His..." I felt sick remembering what Andrea had done. "Gianni's dead. Andrea killed him."

"I had a feeling. So did his wife which is actually why she came to see me. She was afraid for herself and their daughter. I promised my protection in exchange for the information she had."

Teo's phone chimed but he ignored it. "Come on. Let's get you something to eat. Then you can relax in the tub."

"Okay."

After a good meal and a relaxing bath, Teo assured me that Abigail and Maria were settled in, and he carried me to bed.

We climbed into bed, and I laid my head on his chest. With Teo's arms around me, I felt better than I had in all the time since Gabe took me. My body still hurt all over, and my muscles were weak and shaky, but I was back with Teo. He was alive, and I was finally free from Andrea once and for all.

We laid there in the comfortable silence for a long time. After all the craziness that we had been through we both needed some quiet time to just hold each other and be still.

Teo lazily ran his fingertips over my arm and shoulder nearly sending me into a trance with his touch.

The content quiet was broken by the chiming of Teo's phone. He ignored it but a second chime came in. I tilted my head up so that I could look at him.

"If you need to get that..."

"No, it's fine."

"What if it's important? It could be one of the guys."

"Okay." Teo rolled to his side to grab his phone from the nightstand.

He scrolled for a moment, sent a long text back, before returning to his spot with me.

"Everything okay?"

"Yeah. Nic's got us a way back to Italy but we're going to have to split up."

"Split up, why?"

"There's a couple smaller boats leaving separate ports. Neither can carry all of us. Some will leave from the eastern port and sail into Tuscany while the rest of us will travel to the northern tip of Corsica and go from there toward the South of France. We do enough business there that if we fly from Nice to Italy it won't seem unusual."

"A trip to Nice?" I perked up, lifting my head to smile at Teo.

His brow lifted. "Would you like that?"

I tilted my head as if to consider the question. "Hmm. Would I enjoy going back to the place where we first met and fell in love?"

Teo gently tickled my side and I giggled.

"You know..." His sudden seriousness snapped me out of my laughter to listen to him. "We *could* see if my dad, Dario, and Mira could fly out to meet us there."

"Oh," I said, feeling a bit deflated.

"You wouldn't like for them to be there too?"

"I don't know." I shrugged. "Don't get me wrong, I love your family. But I just thought it would be good to get away from it all for a while."

"Well, that's what the honeymoon will be for. I thought it would be nice to have our families at our wedding."

I froze in surprise and pushed myself up onto my elbow to better face Teo. "Wedding?"

"You said before that you liked the idea of a wedding in Nice."

"Yeah. I did. But I thought..."

"We tried it my father's way and that didn't work out. I think it's time we take control of our destiny. So, you still want to marry me?"

"With all my heart."

"Good. Then we will get the majority of the men on the eastern ship. Nic, Dante, Luca, Alessandro, and Enzo will come with us to the Northern port and from there we will meet my father and the rest of the family in Nice."

"That sounds perfect. I'm almost too afraid to get my hopes up after everything that's happened."

"Don't ever be afraid to feel hopeful. I will always do everything within my power to make your dreams come true."

"Oh, Teo." I wrapped my arms around his waist and squeezed.

99

Teo squeezed me back and kissed the top of my head. "Now, let's get some sleep. We have a lot to do tomorrow."

I kissed him once, deeply, before snuggling into the crook of his arm and quickly drifting off to sleep.

Early the next morning, I jolted upright in the bed, screaming as loud as I could. Loose strands of hair clung to my dampened face and my chest heaved as I struggled to pull in enough air. I had dreamed that I was still in Andrea's grasp, that Teo had never rescued me from marrying him. I woke, not knowing which was reality and which had been a dream.

Teo ran into the room in a panic, scanning our surroundings for threats but he calmed when he found me alone in the bed.

"What's wrong? What happened?"

"Nothing. I'm fine. It was just a bad dream." I reassured him but I was trembling. I pulled off the covers and climbed out of bed, trying to act as normal as possible. "Why are you up so early?"

"I was just calling my father to arrange their transport for the wedding."

"Did he seem upset about how we are doing this?"

"Not at all. I think at this point he'll just be glad that it's over with." Teo laughed. "I have to admit, I'm looking forward to the wedding but I'm looking forward to after the wedding even more."

"You mean the honeymoon?" I asked him playfully and he chuckled.

"Well that too but I was actually referring to being married to you."

"How sweet." I wrapped my arms around his waist, letting my head rest on his shoulder, and he wrapped me in his warm embrace.

"Are you hungry? I cooked breakfast."

"You cooked? I didn't know you could cook."

"Just because I don't do it often, doesn't mean that I don't know how. Bianca taught me when I was a boy."

"Wow. A sexy, thoughtful, loving man who can cook? It seems that I really lucked out."

"Don't forget great in bed," Teo smirked and squeezed me a little tighter.

"Oh yes, and we can't forget modest, too," I teased before planting a quick kiss on his lips. "And to answer your question, yes I'd love some breakfast and coffee. Do we have any coffee?"

"Of course, we have coffee." Teo smiled.

"I'm just going to make myself presentable then I'll be right down."

"Don't make me wait too long." Teo kissed me tenderly before heading downstairs.

CHAPTER 14

Teo

After breakfast, Mia and I sat down to talk to Abigail about the plan to get her and Maria out of Corsica.

"Why do we have to go with the other men? I trust Mia. I don't know your men."

"They are all honorable. I trust them completely. I assure you that they will get you somewhere safe per my instructions."

"But why do we have to split up?"

"There isn't enough room on either one of the ships for all of us, so we have to divide our group. We are sending you on the most direct route to get you and Maria out the fastest."

Mia gave Abigail a reassuring smile and squeezed her forearm. "I promise, this is the safest way."

Abigail sighed. "Alright. Thank you for your help."

"Of course."

"Now, we need to hurry if we are going to make the drive before the ship departs. Go grab your things and a few snacks from the kitchen as well. It will be a few hours journey but then you will both be safe." I stood and the three of them followed before hurrying to their rooms.

I followed Mia upstairs to help her gather our things but paused when an incoming message chimed on my phone.

+39 06 373 8001: I've booked a train to Nice. Please don't do anything until we speak.

Guilt gripped my gut as I typed out a reply.

Matteo: I'll text you when we arrive.

+39 06 373 8001: Thank you.

"Everything okay?" Mia asked from the top of the stairs, and I tensed.

"Everything's fine." I slipped my phone back in my pocket before smiling and hurrying up the steps to join her.

After some discussion with Nic and Alessandro, I decided that the best course of action was for us to divide our group into thirds, sending one group East with Abigail and Maria to sail on a ship bound for Tuscany. The second group would go south to *Sardegna* before traveling to the mainland. Andrea's allies would be looking for Mia and they wouldn't expect us to take a ship to Nice when there were so many options to go directly to Italy.

After we packed and said our goodbyes to Abigail and Maria, they accompanied the group of my men going to the Eastern port not far from where we were.

I loaded our supplies and clothes into the back of the SUV and helped Mia climb into the back seat before taking the spot beside her. Luca and Enzo took the front, and we pulled out of the driveway.

There was tension in the car as we all kept our eyes open for anyone that might be following us. I had wished that we could have left out the same day that we had taken down Andrea and his men, before word could have spread, but I was glad that I had helped Abigail and her daughter.

"What are you looking for? Mia asked as I kept my head swiveling from side to side.

"Trying to make sure that we don't have a tail."

"You think someone could be following us?"

"Not right now. But Andrea could have allies that might try to retaliate. I'm sure word has already begun to spread about what went down yesterday."

"I'm sorry. I know that staying the extra day to help Abigail and Maria has complicated things a bit, but I really appreciate you supporting me with wanting to help them."

"I've learned that once you set your mind to something, I might as well help or get out of your way. Besides, it was the right thing to do." I smiled affectionately, wrapping my arm around her shoulders and squeezing her gently to my side.

Her frame felt smaller than the last time I held her in Italy. She's lost weight since being in Corsica. Her eyes were shadowed and her expression even when she was laughing, was weaker. It was something that we would have to talk about sooner or later, but every time I brought it up Mia dismissed it.

She didn't want to talk about it, and I would let her wait, for the time, without pushing. But only because I needed her to hold it together until we were out of Corsica and safely back at our home where I was in control. While we were in a different country on a different crime family's turf, I needed to focus on keeping her safe and getting her out. Once we were home she could fall apart because I would be there to put her back together again.

"You seem quieter than usual." Mia spoke softly so that only I could hear her. "Is everything all right?"

"Everything's fine or at least it will be once we get out of this place for good."

"It seems like there's a lot on your mind."

"I'm just worried about you. I know you've been through hell, and I probably don't even know the half of it."

"Teo..." Mia warned.

"I know you don't want to talk about your time with Andrea and I get it. For now, hold on to those secrets while we focus on getting you out of here but once we're home you're going to have to talk to me about it. I need to know what you went through, and you need to be able to

105

tell someone if you're ever going to be able to heal from it. Promise me when we're home that you'll talk to me."

"Okay. I promise."

As we made our way out of the main city and further North toward the port, we were able to relax a little more, knowing that the chance of someone following us that far out was slim.

"It should only take us about an hour to get from Linguizzetta to Bastia. The port is busy so it should be easy enough to blend in as we make our way to the ferry where we will be boarding using our fake IDs."

"Fake IDs? How did you get those?"

"I have a guy who can falsify just about anything. I had him do a rush order before we left Italy and brought them with me. I had hoped to find a way to get you home that didn't include being smuggled in a cargo hold."

"The ferry does sound better."

"Good. You will be traveling as Genevieve Odette Beaumont, French citizen, married to Julian Lewis Beaumont."

"What about the rest of the men?"

"Unfortunately, fake IDs are a hot commodity and there just wasn't enough time to make one for all of them. They will have to sneak into the luggage compartment and wait out the six-hour trip there."

"I feel bad for them being stuck down in cargo."

"Don't worry, we'll be fine," Enzo assured Mia.

"So, are you two really going to tie the knot this time?" Luca said from the driver's seat as he glanced at us in the rearview mirror.

"That's the plan," I said happily.

"Good. Because I already got dressed up in a tux once for you guys. I've about reached my quota."

"You wear a suit all the time," Mia chimed in.

"A suit and a tux are two very different things if you ask me." Luca smiled at her through the mirror. "Tuxes just feel stuffy to me."

"But they're so sexy," Mia said teasingly.

"Well in that case," Luca smirked in the mirror and glanced back at her. "Maybe I'll have to reconsider wearing one more often."

"Watch it now," I warned with a chuckle.

"Oh, I'm not going to steal your girl. Don't worry. I just mean that maybe if I'm wearing a tux I might attract a girl like her."

I quirked an eyebrow and used a challenging tone. "As if you could steal her away."

"All I'm gonna say is that you're lucky that you're my future don or I might try." Luca winked at Mia through the mirror, and she laughed a warm, real laugh that made me forget the slight pang of jealousy.

Luca's flirtation and jokes were harmless, and it was good to see Mia finding her place among my friends.

We arrived at the port just in time to begin loading onto the ferry. Enzo and Luca join the other men while Mia and I prepared to board. Mia tensed as we walked through the gate with our fake ids. But we passed without a problem and were soon settled on board.

"We have just over six hours before we will be in Nice. We could go swimming or sunbathe at the pool deck."

"I don't think that would be a good idea." Mia looked away from me and began fidgeting with her shirt hem.

"Why not? It could be relaxing to soak up some sun and maybe have a drink."

"I just don't feel up to it if that's okay. Maybe I'll just go try to find a seat somewhere to rest."

"I'm sorry. Of course, you need to rest after everything you've been through. If you want to rest, we have a cabin. Do you need a nap first and we could swim later?"

"I don't even have a swimsuit."

"They have shops on board. I'll buy you any one you want."

"I just don't want to go swimming, okay?" Mia snapped before taking a step back. "I'm sorry I'm just tired. And there's a lot to think about with the wedding. Can we just go to the cabin please?"

"Of course," I said hesitantly and led Mia toward the stairs that led to the cabins.

"I didn't mean to upset you." I studied her as we walked. "I thought you enjoyed swimming like we did on vacation when we were in Nice before."

"I did. I mean I do. I just don't think it's a good idea right now and I don't feel like being out in front of all those people." Mia was acting strange, almost like she was uncomfortable with me, and I didn't like it.

I let her into the cabin and threw our suitcases on the bed. "I'm afraid there's not much in the bags. I mostly brought these for show on the ferry because I couldn't travel with much when sneaking into Corsica. But I can buy you anything you need while we're here."

"As long as there's something for me to sleep in I'm fine. I just want to sleep."

"Okay. But I wouldn't sleep for the whole trip, or you won't be able to sleep tonight."

"I know."

I hesitated before bringing up any other plans, but I had to keep her talking. I had to know what was going on with her and why she was acting so strange. "There's a great restaurant on board. I thought it would be fun to go out to dinner together but after you rest, of course."

"That sounds good, but I guess that means I *will* need something to wear."

"Why don't I go pick out something for you while you rest? I can surprise you with a beautiful dress to wear to dinner tonight."

"That sounds wonderful, but I think I should pick out my own dress. Why don't you stay with me for a little while? I would love to be able to just lay in your arms."

That sounded better to me than anything I had suggested, and I smiled, knowing that she was at least still the Mia that I loved somewhere inside.

"That sounds amazing."

"Good. I'm just going to change."

Mia took out a pair of soft sleep pants and one of my big shirts and took them into the bathroom to change. *When had she gotten so shy?* She wouldn't even change in front of me and that left me even more confused and curious.

Once Mia got out of the bathroom we pulled down the blanket and sheet and she climbed into bed. I climbed in behind her and she snuggled up against me. Before long she was sound asleep. I was just dozing off when my phone chimed. Sleepily, I reached over to the side table and opened the lock screen.

+39 06 373 8001: Train will be arriving tonight. Meet me at the Blue Sapphire at ten.

A sick feeling settled in my stomach, and I wasn't sure if it was because I was hiding something from Mia or if it was because I felt too far out of control of the situation. Maybe it was a little of both.

I put my phone down and tried to fall back asleep, but the strange way Mia had been acting kept nagging at me. She rolled over and draped her arm across me. The hem of my shirt that she wore lifted up a bit on her side and that's when I saw the hint of a bruise spread over her barely exposed flank.

110

I gently lifted her shirt to expose more of her side and back. It took everything I had not to gasp at the dark, angry bruises. No wonder she didn't want to go parading around in a bikini in front of a bunch of strangers at the pool. She probably also wanted to pick out her own dress to make sure that it hid all the marks that bastard had left on her.

I was an idiot for not thinking about it sooner. I laid there for a long time, imagining what she must have gone through and thinking of all the ways I would have loved to drag out Andrea's death.

CHAPTER 15

Teo

After an amazing dinner, followed by a stroll along the deck at sunset, we finally docked in Nice. I'd had a good time with Mia but once we were in port, I had to shift my thoughts to more pressing matters, like making sure that my men were able to disembark without detection.

I escorted Mia away from the crowd of people at the bottom of the loading ramp with our two small suitcases.

"How will we know if they got off the ship okay?" Mia whispered.

"We're supposed to meet them around here." I urged her through the bustling port, heading for an old, dilapidated building.

"What is this place?"

"It used to be a restaurant but there was some fire damage a few months back and the owners haven't rebuilt. I figured it would be an inconspicuous spot to meet up. Come on. Let's get inside."

I cautiously opened the back door and peeked inside. There was no sign of anyone, but I placed my hand on the gun in my waistband just to be safe. I kept Mia close behind me as we entered the old building. The smell of smoke was still thick in the room and several walls had char marks from the fire. I led Mia further into the restaurant, when a sudden movement caught my eye. I pulled my gun quickly and aimed just in time to see my friends holding their hands up with guns gripped firmly.

"Whoa, Teo. It's us." Luca sounded startled.

I lowered my gun with a sigh of relief. "I wasn't expecting you guys to already be here."

"Well, unlike you, we didn't have to worry about checking out, getting our luggage, and all that fancy stuff," Enzo teased.

"So, everyone made it here without being detected?" I looked around, noting that Alessandro, Luca, Enzo, Dante, and Nic were all there along with a handful of men that had joined us.

"All here and accounted for. And we were careful. No one followed us," Alessandro reported.

"Good. My father and the others arrived on the private jet a couple of hours ago. He should be sending us a ride soon. We're just supposed to sit tight until the cars arrive."

I checked my watch. It was nearly seven. I had three hours to be picked up, get Mia settled with my family, and find an excuse to slip out to the Blue Sapphire to meet Anna by ten. I hated all the sneaking around and secrecy. I would be glad once I knew what was going on so that I could take care of whatever it was and get it over with. I was tired of focusing on anything other than Mia and our upcoming wedding.

We only waited for about fifteen minutes before two black SUVs pulled up to the back of the restaurant. My father sent a text letting me know that the cars had arrived for us, and I led the men out.

Half an hour later we pulled up to the same hotel where I had been shot. We had bought that hotel during my stay and still owned it. It was a good investment that brought in a lot of money, but I had always come up with some reason not to go back. Walking through the luxurious lobby, my pulse began to race with memories of that night.

I took a deep breath and did the best that I could to settle my nerves as we walked into my father's hotel suite where the rest of our family had gathered for drinks. My father sat in the living room with Armando, Mira, Vittoria, and Courtney.

After several minutes of greetings with hugs and small talk, the conversation between the girls moved on to our wedding.

"I don't know how we're going to pull it off in just two days," Mia said with some concern in her voice.

"Don't worry about that at all," Mira comforted her with a bright, confident smile. "The girls and I have been very busy ever since we got the call."

"You have?"

"Oh yeah. Since The wedding will be smaller this time around, with less guests, we were able to downsize a bit. And we are planning a big reception when we get home," Courtney stated.

"I found a local quartet to play the ceremony, a florist willing to do a rush job, and Vittoria called in a favor with a photographer she knows."

"Also, I figured your wedding dress may not be available now, so I did something." Vittoria smirked at Mia. "But if you don't like it you can tell me, and we will find something off the rack instead."

"You got me a wedding dress?"

"Got? Hell no. She *made* you a wedding dress," Courtney added.

"An actual real life Vittoria creation? I have to see it." Mia's excited tone made me smile.

"It's hidden away in my room. We can go check it out if you want."

"That sounds great." Mia beamed at Vittoria. "Teo, do you mind?"

I smiled adoringly at her, amused by her excitement, and squeezed her hand. "Of course not. Go.

Have fun and enjoy yourself. I need to run out for a little bit anyway."

Mia was too excited to even think about questioning me as she wrapped her arms around my neck and squealed. I kissed her tenderly before letting her go as all the girls flooded out of the room.

My father raised a curious eyebrow. "Run out? Where are you going?"

Of course, he would notice. Nothing got past him. "I just have a couple of things I need to take care of before I get settled in."

My father understood at least in vague terms. It was part of our business. He studied me for a moment longer before giving a nod. "Once you're back, come to my room for a drink. I'd like to catch up on everything that happened while you were away."

"Of course." I gave a nod before leaving.

It was nine-thirty by the time I walked into the Blue Sapphire's Lounge. I scan the bar for any sign of Anna or anyone that might be setting me up. There were only a couple of patrons scattered at different tables. A couple chatted intimately leaning over the table toward each other and a couple of businessmen sat sipping bourbon near the door. In the back of my mind, I worried that I was being a fool for not bringing along back up. But she had shown me a picture of the two of us together, a picture that I was sure most people wouldn't have readily available. Still, my senses were in high gear, adrenaline pumping through my veins. I didn't like the way this girl had contacted me or how she went about our meeting.

I ordered myself a drink and found a table near the back of the bar. It was perfectly positioned so that my back could be at the corner with a clear view of the door.

I'd only taken a couple of sips of my whiskey when the door opened, drawing my attention to the same girl I'd seen in the texted photograph. Even though it was still warm outside, she carried a jacket draped on her arm along with her purse and a part of me worried that she might be concealing a weapon there. I would have to be cautious either way. I didn't know the woman or who she associated with. She looked nervous as she glanced in my direction and forced a small smile as she headed toward me.

I stood for my chair to greet her as she approached. "Anna, I presume?

"Yes." She flashed a nervous smile.

"Please, have a seat." I pulled out the chair for her, waiting until she sat before rounding to my side of the table.

"You really don't remember me." It was more of a statement than a question, but I shook my head.

"From the photograph I know that you were telling the truth about me knowing you or at least meeting you but I'm sorry I don't."

"Well, in any case, I'm glad you decided to meet me."

"It sounded important."

"It is."

"Well, before we get started, should we get you a drink?" I waved a server to our table and the man hurried over.

"*Bonjour.* Can I get something for you?"

"Just a club soda, *s'il vous plaît.*"

"Of course. Coming right up."

We waited for the server to return before broaching anything more than small talk, like the weather and how her train ride had been. Once she had her drink and the server was out of earshot, I leaned forward with my elbow on the table and lowered my voice.

"So, what was so important that we had to arrange this clandestine meeting?"

Anna took a sip from her glass and let out a sigh before readjusting herself in her seat. "I know you don't remember me, and photos can be altered, but I'm sure you remember the night that picture was taken." I listened intently, wondering why she went straight into defensive mode instead of just telling me whatever it was she had to tell me.

"Why don't you tell me?"

"Your brother had just found out that your father had set up an arranged marriage. He wasn't happy about that and so the two of you were out blowing off steam."

We hadn't exactly been blowing off steam. It was more that Gio was determined to get trashed, and I followed along to keep him out of trouble, but I couldn't expect her to know that.

"Yes. And I remember that I *only* agreed to have two drinks. So how is it that I don't have one memory of you?"

"That I don't know, but I wish I did. The most I can offer is my accounts of that night if you'd care to hear it."

"That would be most helpful, thank you."

"I was out at the club to unwind after a really bad week. I was contemplating leaving because it wasn't really my scene, when you grabbed my hand and pulled me over to the table where you and your brother were. You thought I was a waitress and tried to give me your drink order."

"That sounds mortifying."

"It was actually kind of cute." Anna smiled fondly at the memory. "You apologized and bought me a drink to show that you were sorry. We spent the whole night talking and dancing and flirting."

"Okay, but I don't understand. Why did you seek me out just to relive that night?"

"Because that wasn't the end. After a while of dancing, things began to heat up..." she squirmed in her seat, looking uncomfortable, and a realization hit me.

"Oh, you mean we..." I waved my hand between us, and she nodded.

"You took me up to your brother's VIP suite and we spent the night together."

"And you heard that I was getting married? You thought you'd try to find me, and I'd decide to be with you instead?" Annoyance at the woman's nerve had my tone

119

rising slightly but I forced my volume to remain low enough to keep the conversation between the two of us. "Why would I choose you over my fiancée? The woman I love."

"Because I'm pregnant," she blurted out and my jaw dropped as my brain rushed to catch up.

"No. That was months ago."

"Sixteen weeks, actually. I didn't know who you were until I saw your wedding announcement and when the wedding fell through, I thought it was fate. I knew I had to find you and tell you."

"I don't believe you." I wasn't sure if it was true that I didn't believe her or just denial but either way I felt anger bubbling up inside me at this woman who decided to come into my life and turn everything upside down. Rationally, I knew that if it was true, it wasn't her fault or at least no more than it was mine, but a part of me blamed her for messing everything up, right when everything was about to fall into place with Mia.

Anna removed the jacket that had been draped across her lap and stood up, exposing the smallest little bump to her otherwise flat belly. "Do you still think that I'm lying?"

CHAPTER 16

Mia

I stood there with my mouth hanging open, excitement bubbling up inside me as I stared at the most beautiful wedding dress I had ever seen.

Vittoria peaked around from behind it where she was holding it up and grinned. "Do you like it?"

"Like it? No. I love it." I grinned at her. "This is incredible. How did you possibly pull it off?"

"Absolutely no sleep and lots of espresso."

"I want to say that you shouldn't have but I'm so thrilled that you did." I hugged Vittoria around her neck, and she laughed happily.

"Okay, okay. Enough of that. Go try it on. I want to see you in this dress," Mira exclaimed excitedly.

Vittoria handed me the dress and Mira shooed me into the back room.

I hurriedly stripped down and slipped on my wedding gown, excited to try on such a gorgeous dress. I ran my hands over the intricate beadwork on the bodice and admired the elegant fabric that flared at my waistline. I grinned to myself, all thoughts of the horrors I'd endured far from my mind.

I lightly gripped the flowy silhouette, admiring the way the delicate fabric swayed as I moved. Vittoria had truly outdone herself.

"Mia. Come on. I can't take the waiting," Vittoria called out excitedly from the other side of the door.

I hurried out with a huge grin on my face. "Okay, okay."

The girls all grinned excitedly when I walked out.

"Oh, Mia. You look beautiful," Mira said in awe.

122

"Come, you can get a better look over here." Vittoria pulled me over in front of a full length mirror.

SI stood there, staring at the most beautiful wedding gown I'd ever seen. The lines fit my curves perfectly, making me feel like a mix between a supermodel and a princess.

"Vittoria, it's incredible."

I twisted from side to side to view the full dress.

"Mia, you look amazing."

"That dress is perfect for you."

"You are gorgeous."

The mix of compliments flooded from the group, and I beamed at myself in the mirror. I was practically glowing.

"You need to see the beadwork and lace on the back. It's very elegant," Vittoria said.

Courtney rushed to hand me a smaller mirror. I scooped my hair and brushed it over one shoulder as I looked into the small mirror to see the larger mirror's reflection.

There was a collective gasp from all four of us. All the breath rushed from me, and I felt like the floor was opening up to swallow me whole. The air was suddenly too thick to breathe, like a dense smog had settled into the room.

The middle of the dress had a large cut out, exposing angry black, blue, and green bruises and half-healed lash marks covering my back.

Tears burned my eyes and I felt like I might throw up.

Before I could say anything, Mira and Vittoria were by my side, steadying me, while Courtney took the mirror from my trembling hands.

"It's okay," Vittoria said in a rush. "I can fix it."

"How?" My voice quivered. "Makeup isn't going to cover that, not completely."

"Mia, are you sure that you should be getting married so soon after everything that's happened? I'm sure if you just explain to Teo..." Mira asked gently, taking my hands in hers and meeting my eye.

"No. Andrea has already taken so much from us. I won't let him take another moment." I fought back tears.

"We can fix this. Just hear me out." Vittoria paused before continuing. "We can use makeup to at least fade it and I brought some extra fabric. I can use the same lace to cover the back so it will hide the bruises while adding an elegant detail."

"Vittoria, thank you. Thank you so much." I hugged her, tears welling up in my eyes as Mira and Courtney joined us in a group hug.

A sudden knock on the door put our embrace to a stop and Vittoria turned to answer.

"Who is it?"

"It's me. I need to see Mia." Teo's voice came through the door, and I tensed.

"Wait, you can't come in. She's trying on her wedding dress," Vittoria called through the door before turning to shoo me off toward the bedroom. "Go change."

I hurried into the bedroom and changed back into my regular clothes before quickly returning to the main room.

"Are you ready for the wedding?" I could hear Courtney ask Teo as I neared the room.

"Of course." He didn't sound as excited as I expected.

"Vittoria made Mia an amazing dress. Just wait until you see it. It's gorgeous and Mia looks amazing in it."

"I'm sure Mia will look great." Teo said flatly, almost sounding bored and I had to admit that it hurt.

I thought he would at least be a little excited. "Mira, can I speak with you for a moment, outside?"

"Of course."

I heard the door open and shut before I walked into the room. "Where'd Teo run off to?"

"He just stepped outside with Mira. Must be some family business," Vittoria said with a shrug.

"Oh, okay. I want to thank you again for the dress. It is gorgeous."

"I'm happy you like it. I'll make the alterations after dinner so you can try it on again tomorrow."

Teo walked back into the room with Mia and a flash of something that looked like guilt crossed his face before he quickly replaced it with a smile.

"*Ciao, bellissima.*"

I wasn't sure what was going on, but I pushed it from my mind and focused on my handsome fiancé standing in front of me. "*Ciao*, Teo. What a wonderful surprise. I wasn't sure what time you'd be finished with your errands. But I'm glad that you are already back."

"Unfortunately, I can't stay. I only stopped by to let you know that my errands are going to take longer than expected. So, I may not be able to make it back for dinner."

"Oh, okay." Teo was acting odd. He hadn't felt that distant from me in a long while and I hated the reminder of it. Especially after everything we'd just gone through and with the wedding so close.

"I'm going to go check in with my father, then I'll be off. I'm sorry, Mia." The weight of those words left a sickening feeling settling into the pit of my stomach. There was something about the way he said he was sorry, like he was apologizing for a lot more than having to run a few errands.

"And we have a full day tomorrow," Mira added.

My brow furrowed, and I turned to face her. "We do?"

"We have your final dress fitting, remember? Plus, I was going to surprise you with a spa day so that you could be relaxed and refreshed for your special day."

"That would be nice." I looked at Teo apologetically. "I guess that means the next time we see each other will be at our wedding."

"Well, you always like the idea of me not getting to see you before the wedding. I guess you'll be getting your wish then won't you?" Teo smiled but it didn't reach his eyes and I couldn't shake the feeling that something wasn't right.

I stepped forward and took his hands in mine, looking up into his eyes and searching for answers that he wasn't willing to share. "Are you sure everything's all right?"

"Of course." He reached up and brushed his thumb over my cheek, warming me as he cupped my face. "There's nothing for you to worry about."

"Okay."

"I love you."

"I love you too." Still uneasy and desperate to feel a connection to him, I softly pressed my lips to his and he returned it with a gentle kiss.

"I'm sorry. I really have to go.".

"It's okay. You take care of business now because in two days you're all mine." I forced my doubts out of my mind and smiled, reassured slightly by the smile Teo returned.

That feeling didn't last as Teo cast me a regretful look before turning to walk out the door.

CHAPTER 17

Teo

I hated lying to Mia. I could stare down the barrel of an enemy's gun and lie without breaking a sweat, but one glance into those deep, brown eyes and my resolve crumbled.

In two days, I was supposed to stand at an altar on a cliff overlooking the Verdon Gorge and vow to love, honor, and cherish the woman I wanted nothing more than to spend the rest of my life with. But before I could do that, I had to find out the truth about Anna.

If she was lying about me being the father, then I would deal with her, and Mia would never have to hear about any of it. But if it was true and Anna was carrying my child, I had to know.

I pulled out my phone as I made a beeline for my rental car.

"*Ciao,* Teo," Alessandro answered quickly.

"Has everything been arranged?

"*Sì.* The lab technician had already gone home for the night, but we were able to persuade him to come back to the lab."

"And the girl? Has she given you any trouble?"

"She wasn't thrilled. She wanted to go home for the night. Said this could wait till tomorrow but I impressed upon her the importance of her complying with your wishes."

"Good. I'll be there in fifteen. Tell the lab tech to get everything ready. I want this thing done as soon as I get there and give my sample." I hurried my footsteps, nearly running the short distance left to my car. My phone was already on the key fob and hit the unlock button before I was within reach of my door.

"You got it. The actual test doesn't take that long to come through. Especially with a lab tech as motivated as ours."

"Good. Because I don't have any time to waste. I want to be standing at that altar, watching Mia walk down the aisle with a clear head and a clear conscience, knowing that that isn't my baby."

There was a hesitation on the other end of the line, and I could tell that Alessandra wanted to say something, but he was holding back. "Go ahead Alex. What are you wanting to say?"

"You said she had a picture. Is there any chance..?"

"That night was a blur. I remember waking up the next morning with the worst hangover I've ever had but I could have sworn that I only had two drinks. I never liked to cut loose when I was with Gio."

"I know. You said you didn't trust him enough."

"I had the smallest suspicion that my drink had been drugged but I had no way of proving it. The only person that was close to my drink was the bartender and Gio. I had no real reason to think that he would drug me."

"He was always complaining that you needed to loosen up. Maybe he took it into his own hands."

I let out a heavy sigh. "In any case, I guess there is a chance. Especially if I was drugged."

"Well, let's just hope that one night wasn't enough to do any permanent damage."

"Yeah. I'm not sure how Mia would handle a complication like that. I'll just be glad once all this is over."

"I'll get things started on my end. Come through the side entrance when you get here. The door will be unlocked."

"I'm already on my way so I should be there soon."

The fifteen-minute drive only took ten. I was eager to get the whole ordeal out of the way. I parked my car around back next to Alessandro's rental and entered through the side door.

The building wasn't large and entering from the side put me in some kind of storage area, but I easily followed the agitated voices to the adjacent room that opened up into an ultra-modern lab.

"*Ciao,*" I said firmly as I looked over to Anna arguing with Alessandro. "What's the problem here?"

"The problem is that I don't like needles. You can't force me to get this done."

I narrowed my eyes at her and took the three strides to where she was standing with her arms crossed, pouting like a spoiled child. I towered over her, but I didn't let her small frame deter me from using the intimidatingly cold tone I usually reserved for my enemies. "You were the one who contacted me, remember?"

Anna opened her mouth to argue but I didn't let her. "You are the one demanding that I believe that I'm the father of this child even though I have no memory of being with you."

"This baby *is* yours."

"Then sit down, shut up, and let this nice technician take your blood. He's already working after hours which…" I turned my attention to the wide-eyed lab technician dressed in scrubs and a white lab coat. "I will be paying you triple your usual rate."

He gave me an appreciative nod and Anna reluctantly sat to have her blood taken.

Once he was done with Anna, I removed my coat and sat in the seat on the other side of his metal tray. I unbuttoned my cuff and began rolling up my sleeve, but the technician looked at me curiously.

"Alright, I'm ready to get this over with."

"I'm sorry, sir. The father—"

"Alleged father," I corrected him. I wasn't sure why I'd felt the need to clarify that I might not be the father, but I did.

He nodded nervously. "The *alleged* father just needs a simple cheek swab."

"Oh." I rolled my sleeve back down, feeling slightly embarrassed at my lack of knowledge on the subject.

"If you'll just open wide..."

I did as he asked, and he quickly collected the sample.

"All done."

"Good. Thank you. How long does it take to get the results in?"

"Probably Monday."

"That's unacceptable. I'm getting married the day after tomorrow."

"I can...put a rush on it but the earliest it will be is mid-day tomorrow."

"Okay. Alessandro, have one of your men posted with him until we get the test results in. I'm the only one to find out the results. And have another man keep an eye on Anna to make sure she doesn't disappear on us before we find out the truth."

"*Si, Signore.*"

"I do not need one of your goons leering at me all night," Anna huffed.

"No. But I do."

"All this stress isn't healthy for the baby. *Your* baby."

"As far as the stress, you brought that on yourself when you contacted me. If you are telling the truth then you have nothing to be worried about. As for the latter, whether or not that baby is mine has yet to be determined."

"I—" I didn't let Anna continue. Until I had answers about the paternity of her baby there was nothing I wanted to hear from her. There'd be plenty to talk about once the test results were in one way or the other. I turned to Alessandro. "You got this?"

"Yeah. We'll take care of it all."

I gave him a confirming nod before turning away and walking out the door. I made it out to my car, planning to go back to the hotel and hide away for the rest of the night. We'd ended earlier than expected but I couldn't be around Mia until I knew the truth. There would be no way that I could keep this from her if I was around her and I didn't want to worry her about something that might be nothing at all.

I climbed in my car and revved the engine as I pulled out of the parking lot and headed to The Blue Sapphire. I couldn't risk running into Mia or someone else from the wedding party, but I needed a drink, and it was somewhere that no one would know me. I could drink alone, surrounded by people. I didn't feel like sitting alone in my hotel, but I didn't feel like talking either.

There were a few more patrons than when I had been there before. Since I didn't need the privacy of a table, I took a seat at the bar and waved for the bartender to bring me a drink.

I finished my second drink and signaled the bartender to bring me a third when a knockout walked up to the bar and took a seat next to me.

"Sauvignon Blanc, *s'il vous plaît.*" I glanced over to her, and she offered a soft smile.

I tipped my head and lifted my glass before taking a drink, losing myself in my thoughts again the moment I turned my gaze from her.

"Are you here for business or pleasure?" Her sultry tone jarred me from my thoughts.

"Excuse me?"

"Business or pleasure? Or maybe a bit of both?" She practically purred as she leaned a little closer to me and took another sip from her wine glass.

"A wedding actually," I stated bluntly. I had no interest in carrying on a conversation with some random woman at the bar but there was no reason to be rude either.

"Ah, let me guess, you're the best man?" She smiled, lightly placing her hand on my forearm.

"Actually, I'm the groom," I said coolly while slowly pulling my arm out from under her hand.

I expected her to look flustered or apologetic at least but she seemed unaffected by the information. In fact, her smile broadened ever so slightly. "When is the wedding?"

I raised a curious brow, wondering what she was up to and why she wasn't ending the conversation to move on to the next lonely businessman in the bar.

"The day after tomorrow."

Her expression brightened and her tone lifted. "Then we are both in luck."

"How so?"

"Because" she leaned in closer, her hand resting on my bicep, and she lowered her voice. "Now you have the opportunity for one last dalliance before you tie the knot."

I pulled back and gently removed her hand from my arm. "Thanks for the offer. But I'm not interested."

"A one-woman man? Such a rarity these days. But an admirable trait, nonetheless." She downed the rest of her wine in one gulp and put the money on the bar before taking her leave.

Finally, alone, I ordered another drink and lost myself in the worries of the day. Tomorrow my entire life could change with one simple little test. It wasn't that I didn't want children, heirs. But not from some one-night stand that I couldn't even remember because my brother most likely had roofied me in some attempt to make me loosen up.

I wanted children with Mia when the time was right, when it would be a happy occasion that we could celebrate together and not a complication that put our wedding and our marriage in jeopardy.

I sat at the bar drinking until late into the night. I drank more than I had in a long time, but nothing seemed to calm the nagging worry that kept creeping into my mind.

What if this is the end for Mia and me?

CHAPTER 18

Mia

After Teo left, I couldn't shake the uneasy feeling I got when he apologized for having to handle business that evening. While the other girls fluttered around the room, talking about the last-minute wedding plans, my mind kept drifting back to Teo.

Something was definitely off but I wasn't sure what. I hoped there wasn't anything serious wrong that Teo was trying to shield me from. I'd been through a lot at the hands of Andrea Romano, and the nightmares still haunted me, but I was healing. It helped to know that he was dead, and I was still alive. I had survived. It was something I reminded myself of every time the horrors of what he'd done crept into my mind.

Could Teo be getting cold feet? The fear crossed my mind, but he seemed so sure and so eager for us to get married it was hard to imagine that that might be the case.

"Mia did you hear anything that I just said?" Courtney studied with a puzzled expression.

"What? Sorry."

"What's on your mind? You've seemed out of it for the last hour."

"I was just thinking about Teo." Technically it wasn't a lie, but the girls smiled fondly, unaware of my concerns.

"Of course, you were," Vittoria said with a smile. "You guys have waited and been through so much. Just think, in a day and a half you two will finally be married."

"I know. I'm so excited."

"Then why don't you sound it?" Mira looked at me concerned.

"I guess it's just that we've been through so much it doesn't seem like it's really going to happen." I hadn't realized that the thought had even crossed my mind until I was looking for an excuse, but it was true. I was worried that it might not happen. But I wanted it to, more than anything. I loved Teo. I always had. I wanted to spend the rest of my life as his wife and partner.

"Well," Vittoria started as she rose from the couch. "I've got some alterations to a wedding dress that are not going to sew themselves, so I'm off. I will see you ladies in the morning."

My phone chimed and I pulled it out of my purse. There was a message from a blocked number.

RESTRICTED: Seems the future don is hard at work tonight. [Image 1 Attachment]

I clicked to open the attached image, curious at what it might be. I thought perhaps Teo was out having a drink with the guys. But I never expected to see a picture of him sitting at a bar with a beautiful woman leaning in to whisper in his ear, her hand so lovingly draped on his arm in a comfortable, familiar pose.

I felt as if the ground might open up and swallow me whole and my stomach roiled. *Could it really be that he was cheating?* Just two days before our wedding after everything we had been through could I really believe that he would do that to me?

The proof is right in front of you. My brain reminded me. In truth, although I felt like I really knew Teo for my entire life, I had only known him for a few months all together. Could he really be so different from what I believed?

"Since Teo isn't going to be joining you for dinner, why don't we go out somewhere? French cuisine is delicious even if it's not something you would want all the time," Courtney asked.

"I'm actually pretty worn out. I've been through a lot the past few days. I was thinking that it might be a good idea to turn in early, maybe order some room service, and just watch some television before bed."

"Are you sure?" Courtney sounded disappointed.

"Mia's right," Mira said. "She's been through a lot, and we don't want her to overdo it before the wedding."

"Or before the honeymoon," Courtney added with a playful smirk.

"Ugh," Mira groaned. "You're talking about my brother."

"Oh, you know it's true. We're all adults here and I'm sure that we all know what a honeymoon's for." They laughed but my smile was hollow.

"You ladies have a good night." I smiled and stood, offering each of them a hug before gathering my purse and heading for the door.

I couldn't get to my hotel room fast enough. I wasn't sure if I wanted to fall apart or explode with anger but neither one needed to be done in front of Mira and Courtney.

When I got to my room, I pulled out my phone again and took one more look at the photograph before dialing Teo's number. It went straight to voicemail. I tried again but it went to voicemail again.

"Teo, it's me. We need to talk. Call me as soon as you get this."

I managed to keep my voice calm, though I had no idea how, and I hung up the phone before breaking down into tears. I cried for several minutes before convincing myself that maybe it wasn't as bad as it seemed. I pulled out the picture again to see if it really had been that bad. Her perfectly manicured hands gently gripped his biceps as she leaned forward. Her face was blocked by his, but she was close enough that her lips could have been pressed

141

against his cheek or brushing against his ear as she whispered sweet nothings or sensual fantasies in his ear.

She was dressed in an elegant little black dress with expensive heels and perfect curves.

She looked like every man's fantasy and there she was clinging to mine. And he wasn't pushing her away. He wasn't pulling back or looking uncomfortable in any way. How long had it been going on for the sender to have time to pull out their phone and take a picture? It couldn't have been one brief moment.

I no longer had an appetite so instead I stripped out of my clothes and stepped into the nearly scalding shower to let the hot water wash away days of horror along with the new nightmares that were sure to come. I cried so hard that I didn't think I would be able to breathe and slid down the shower tiles to sit on the floor as the water pummeled my body. Eventually, the water turned cold, and I began to shiver before even realizing. I pulled myself up off the tiles and turned off the water, wrapping myself in a towel, and stepping out of the shower.

I continued to cry so long that I finally ran out of tears. I no longer felt the pain of betrayal from seeing Teo with another woman. That pain was replaced by a cold numbness. I moved around my hotel room like a robot on autopilot as I dressed for bed and climbed under the covers.

I laid in bed, staring off into the darkness with no more tears to cry when a chill of loneliness began to seep in.

If Teo really was cheating on me could I end things? Could I walk away and risk losing everything? Would my heart let me?

If Teo was cheating on me then everything that I was mourning the loss of, I'd never truly had. The photograph was clear. They say a picture is worth a thousand words, but I only needed three. Teo was cheating.

I barely slept the whole night, unable to shake the uneasy feeling of leaving things unsettled with Teo. I was upset and hurt. My heart shattered into a million pieces at the thought that he would care so little for me that he could cheat on me.

I had to be strong. I would demand that he not go through with taking my family's estate because he broke his vow to me to be loyal and never hurt me. It may not have been in the contract, but I felt like Teo would respect me enough to let me out of the contract. Then again the Teo I thought I knew was not the Teo he was if he had it in him to cheat.

I got up early the next morning finally giving up on trying to sleep but I needed to talk to someone before I confronted Teo. I went to Vittoria's room and knocked on the door. It didn't take long before she answered.

"Mia, what are you doing here so early? Is everything all right?"

"Yeah. I'm sorry did I wake you?"

"No, I was already up and just about to have some breakfast." Vittoria stepped aside and allowed me to enter. "Are you hungry? I ordered plenty."

"Thank you, but I'm not really hungry. Coffee would be nice, though. I didn't get much sleep last night."

"Too excited about your big day?" Her brow furrowed as she studied my expression. "Or is it something else?"

I didn't answer and she led me to a small two-person table where her breakfast and coffee sat. "Please help yourself."

"Thank you." I sat at the table and poured myself a cup of coffee while Vittoria took her seat.

"So, what's going on? I know that there's something wrong."

"What gave me away?"

"I've known you my whole life. I know when there's something on your mind and from the look of you, this is a doozy."

I let out a sigh and took a sip of my coffee before taking out my phone. I pulled up the texted image and handed the phone to Vittoria.

She studied the screen for a moment before looking back up at me, enraged. "What the hell is this? Is that bastard really cheating on you?"

"I don't know. It doesn't make any sense to me at all. Teo has been wonderful. He risked everything to save me and...it just doesn't make sense. Maybe the image could be a fake?"

"A really fucking good fake," Vittoria added.

"Is there any chance it was photoshopped?" I asked with hope, lifting my voice.

"Doubtful but you never know. I know a guy who could check but it might take him a few days to get back to me."

"I don't have a few days. I'm supposed to be marrying Teo tomorrow."

"Then there's only one way to find out with such tight time constraints."

"What's that?"

"Talk to him about it." She handed me back the phone.

"You make it sound like it's so easy."

"It is, or at least it should be with the person you're marrying."

"You're right. And, I have to know the truth or there's no way I can stand up there and vow to be with him forever."

I pulled up the texts between Teo and myself so that I could send him a message, not trusting my voice to not give anything away.

Mia: I need to see you before the girls and I head to the spa.

Teo: Is everything okay?

Mia: Yes. But I need to meet.

Teo: I've got an appointment at eleven. I can meet you at one.

Mia: I need to see you before then. Where are you now?

Teo: I'm just leaving the hotel.

Mia: Wait in your room. I'll meet you there. It won't take long, and you'll have plenty of time to make it to your appointment.

I glanced from my phone to Vittoria. "He's making excuses not to see me. He's still at the hotel but he's about to leave. I need to hurry but I'll be back after."

"Of course. Go." Vittoria shooed me.

I gave her a quick nod before standing from the table and hurrying out of the room as another text came through. I glanced down at my phone, but I barely slowed down as I hurried toward his room.

Teo: I don't have a lot of time right now. I'm supposed to meet Alessandro before my eleven o'clock meeting. I'm already walking out the door. We can meet after.

I debated whether to respond back again. Each text slowed me down and it was obvious that I wasn't going to convince Teo to wait on me. It was strange how adamant he was about not meeting. It only made the worry gnawing at my gut intensify. But my texts were delaying him too. I hit the little microphone button on my phone screen and spoke what I wanted to text as I broke out into an all-out run toward Teo's room.

Mia: Please? It's important and it can't wait.

I turned the corner toward the hall where Teo's room was. He stood just outside his hotel room, looking down at his phone while his free hand anxiously scrubbed at the back of his neck before he typed out a message.

Teo: I'm already in my car. We'll talk later.

I looked up from the text before looking back at Teo. He stared at me like a deer in the headlights. He'd lied to me. He hadn't just avoided me, or acted strangely, he outright lied about being in his car. He wanted to avoid seeing me so bad that it caused him to lie to me and that knowledge stung.

I let the pain fuel my anger. At the lie. At the picture. At what it all most likely meant. I stormed over to Teo, but he didn't move. He didn't take his gaze off of me either.

"What are you doing here?" Teo kept his voice low.

"I told you that I needed to talk to you." I struggled to keep my tone even, but a bit of a bite slipped out.

Teo's face hardened at my tone. "And I told you that I had an appointment to get to and that we'd talk later."

"You also told me that you were already in your car so I think we can both agree that just because you say something doesn't make it true."

"I knew you weren't going to let this go unless you thought I was already in the car and I'm heading to the car now. I can't be late."

"Is this really how you want to spend the day before we're supposed to be getting married? With lies and secret meetings?"

"No. But I have something I *have* to handle. I promise that as soon as I'm done with my meetings, we can talk."

"Did you have a meeting last night, too?"

"Last night?"

"Yeah, at some hotel bar?"

"How—?"

"That doesn't matter. Answer the question."

Teo's startled expression faded into his usual calm, business face. "Yes. Last night our meeting was cut short, so we are meeting today to finalize everything."

"To finalize this?" I pulled up the photo of him with the woman from the bar and held the screen mere inches from his face.

Teo looked stunned and the color faded from his cheeks before his surprise turned to anger. "Did you follow me?"

"What?" I dropped the phone to my side. "No. I didn't follow you. I had no reason to suspect anything, until I saw this."

"Then how the hell did you get a picture of me at the bar?"

"That doesn't matter. How can you be mad at me for having a picture of you, even if I *had* followed you and taken it myself. You're cheating on me."

"Cheating? I'm not—" As the volume of our voices rose, a few other hotel guests began looking our way. Teo opened his hotel door and led me inside before we caused even more of a scene.

Teo gripped me by both shoulders, holding me in place to look at him. "Mia, I promise you that I am not cheating on you. It's not what it looks like. I don't know how you got that picture but what it doesn't show is the second later when I pulled away from her and made it very clear that I wasn't interested.

"Then why are you meeting with her again today?"

"I'm not meeting with her. I wasn't able to complete my meeting last night, so I went to have a drink at the bar when she hit on me. Nothing happened, she hit on me. I turned her down and she left. That was it."

"So, you aren't cheating on me?" Relief flooded me, but I was reluctant to celebrate until I had more answers.

"No, I'm not cheating on you. Trust me, you are the only woman I ever want or need. I swear to you, Mia."

"Then why wouldn't you meet with me? Why go as far as lying to avoid talking to me?"

"Because I knew if I saw you that I wouldn't be able to leave and I would have to throw you over my shoulder and drag you back into my hotel room so that I could have my way with you."

"I don't see the problem...." I smirked, excited by the picture Teo had painted.

"The problem is that I have to make it to a very important appointment, and I can't be late. I'm sorry that I lied but you weren't taking no for an answer."

He was right. I'd been so desperate to speak with him that I ignored everything he said.

"You're right. I'm sorry that I pushed you until you felt like you had to lie to me just to get me to back off."

"I understand why you were desperate for us to talk after seeing that picture."

"Yeah..."

Teo looked down at his watch and back to me apologetically. "I'm so sorry, Mia but I really do have to go. Why don't we meet up a little while later once you're done at the spa, before the wedding rehearsal?"

"It's okay, I just needed to ask you about the photo, but you already answered me about that. I'm not sure how late the spa will run, then I have to get ready, so I'll just see you at the rehearsal."

"Okay, but I really want us to have some time to talk before tomorrow."

I forced a smile and gave a soft nod. Teo seemed to have all the answers, but my gut still told me that something was off. I just had no good reason for it.

CHAPTER 19

Mia

I still felt off for the rest of the day and even at the spa with the girls, surrounded by everything relaxing, I found myself unable to stop thinking about the picture or Teo's strange behavior.

Another thought teased the edges of my mind. Who sent the picture and why?

It was a question I was afraid would go unanswered, but another part was afraid that I'd find out the hard way. With our spa day complete and everything for the wedding in place, all I had to do was to get ready for dinner that night. After changing into a cream and gold cocktail dress, I touched up my lipstick, and headed for the door.

Everyone was getting ready in their own rooms, and we planned to meet at the venue, so I was startled when I opened my door to see Teo standing in the hall.

"Shit. Teo, you scared me to death."

"I'm sorry. I thought we could drive together to the gorge for rehearsal."

"Sure. That would be nice."

I locked my door and let Teo lead me to his car. He helped me into the car before heading around to his side.

Another car pulled into the parking spot beside us, coming to a rough stop. Before Teo opened his door to get in, a woman jumped out of the car and rushed around to him. I watched the whole scene play out like one of those silent movies as she began motioning with her hands and Teo did the same.

Finally, I couldn't take it any longer. I climbed out and rounded the car to stand by Teo's side.

"Teo, what's going on?"

"Nothing. Just get back in the car."

"Are you his fiancée?" She asked with an edge to her voice.

I crossed my arms and cocked my head to one side. "Yes. And who are you?"

"I'm the mother of his unborn child." She placed a hand on her stomach and that's when I noticed the small, rounded bump that was mostly hidden by her flowy blouse.

"Mother—?" The word caught in my throat. My brain couldn't even process what she was saying.

152

DEVOTED TO THE ENEMY

"Yes. Teo and I are going to have a baby together, but he doesn't even want to claim his own child because he's afraid of what you would think. What kind of woman would keep a child from his or her own father?"

"I have no idea what you're talking about."

The woman looked back at Teo in surprise. "You haven't even told her about our child?" She looked offended and placed her hand over her baby bump protectively.

"There's nothing to tell. That is not my child."

"I wasn't with anyone but you. I was completely loyal. So then tell me, Teo. How did I get pregnant? Immaculate conception?"

"Don't be facetious. If you were willing to hook up with me in the back of some club, who knows how many guys you slept with around the same time?"

I whirled around to face Teo in surprise. "Wait, so you did sleep with her?"

"Maybe. I'm not sure."

I slowed my words, enunciating each syllable, careful to make sure that there was no misunderstanding. "You're not sure if you slept with her?"

"No. I don't really remember much from that night, but we can talk about this later."

"Later? Like when? On our honeymoon?" My voice rose with anger. "When were you going to tell me that you might be a father?"

"I'm not the father."

"Yes, you are. I don't care what that stupid test says. This is your child that I'm carrying. Your child that I'm struggling to support."

"You want money? Is that what this is all about? Fine. I'll give you a hundred thousand euros if it will get you to go away."

"You'd really pay me off so that you didn't have to be a part of your child's life?"

"That baby is not mine," Teo roared.

"Stop. All this cannot be healthy for the baby." I stepped forward to try to defuse the situation.

"Obviously your fiancée cares more about your child than you do. And she's right. None of this is healthy for the baby, our baby. I have to go. I thought you were a good man, but you are not the man I thought you were when we first met."

The woman stormed back to her car, got inside and slammed the door shut.

"Good, finally." Teo said angrily as he turned back to the car.

"Teo, you aren't really going to let her go like that are you? She's so upset. She shouldn't be driving."

"She needs to go and leave us alone. Besides, we're going to be late for the rehearsal." As he said the words, the woman pulled out of the parking lot.

"Rehearsal? How can you expect us to just go about our rehearsal like nothing happened when I just found out that you may or may not be a father?"

Teo turned harshly to face me. "I'm not the father. That baby's not mine. Who knows how many men she fucked besides me, if we even did. I'm not convinced that I slept with her. Besides, I always use protection."

"Not always."

"What the hell are you talking about?"

"That night, at the hotel five years ago. We were both so caught up in the moment..."

"You're not saying...you didn't...?"

"No. I didn't but that doesn't mean that I didn't have to worry about it for the few weeks after that, on top of worrying about whether or not you were alive or if I'd ever see you again. So, if you can't tell me that you are one hundred percent sure you didn't sleep with her, then you can't tell me that there's not a chance that she's carrying your child."

"I'm not having this conversation out here in the middle of the parking lot. We're going to be late. Let's go."

He placed his hand on the small of my back to usher me back to my side of the car, but I jerked away. "No. I need answers."

"Mia, get in the fucking car and let's go."

Teo grabbed me by my upper arm and dragged me around to the passenger side of the car. I tried to pull away as he opened the door and shoved me inside, but it was no use. I didn't have a good reason not to just get in the car. I could get just as many answers out of him when we weren't in a parking lot where he was worried about being overheard, so I stayed put as he hurried to his side of the car and climbed in.

We were on the road for at least fifteen minutes before Teo broke the tense silence.

"I'm sorry," he blurted out, barely glancing my way before returning his eyes to the road.

"For which part? For the picture? For letting me find out about the baby this way instead of just being honest with me and telling me the minute you found out?"

A sickening feeling knotted in my stomach. I wanted to know what it was that he was sorry for but at the same time, I feared that, no matter how badly I wanted to forgive him, it would be something that would change our lives forever.

I swallowed around the lump in my throat and took a nervous breath. "Tell me the truth."

"I lied to you when I said that there was nothing going on."

"Lied how?"

"I wasn't handling business. Well, I was but it was personal business."

"What are you saying, Teo?"

"I didn't plan to tell you now, like this. Should I pull over?"

"I don't know. Maybe? I guess it depends on how bad the news is."

I had hoped that he would say it wasn't a big deal and keep driving but instead, he gave a nod and pulled onto the side of the road before unbuckling so that he could turn to face me.

"Before I saw you again at that meeting with Gio and my father, Gio found out that he was going to be married to the future donna Monticelli and that's all I knew of you. He wasn't happy about it. He wanted to blow off some steam, so I tagged along to make sure he didn't take things too far."

156

I listened quietly, only nodding every now and then so that he knew I was listening.

"I made a point to only drink two drinks while I was there. That's why the next day, when I woke up with a massive hangover, and little memory of my night, I was suspicious."

"You'd been drugged?"

"I suspected Gio had slipped something into my drink, but I couldn't prove it. There wasn't any real need to. He was my brother, and he was going to be my don. It was my own fault for not keeping a better eye on my drink."

"Still, I can't believe that he would have drugged you. And why would he?"

"He was always complaining that I was wound too tight and that I should relax. I guess maybe he thought he was helping me cut loose."

"That's still not a good reason."

"Oh, I know. I don't pretend to understand why my brother did the things that he did."

"But I don't understand, what does this have to do with anything?"

"While we were in Corsica I was contacted by a woman who was there that night. She even sent a picture of me and her at the club."

"Why was she contacting you all these months later?"

"She'd seen our wedding announcement in the paper."

"What did she want?"

"To meet with me. She claimed she had something important to talk about."

"And that was her at the bar?"

"No. That really was just a solicitation that I ignored."

"Okay, then you didn't meet with her?"

"No, I met with her."

"So, you met with her then wound up having your picture taken with another woman hitting on you? That seems odd."

Teo nodded and continued. "She told me that she was pregnant. And she claimed that it was mine."

"You said that you didn't remember sleeping with her?" I barely got the words out.

"That night was really fuzzy. If I did sleep with her, then I don't remember it thanks to Gio's roofie."

"And you're going to have a baby...with another woman."

"No. She claimed the baby was mine but it's not. That was the meeting I was going to yesterday and again today. I had someone run a paternity test on the baby to see if he or she is mine."

A wave of relief washed over me. I realized that Teo had a past and sleeping with another woman during the five years we were apart wasn't unexpected but the idea of him having a baby with someone else would have been a lot to process.

"So why is she still saying that the baby is yours?"

"I'm not sure. Denial maybe? Or maybe she is looking for a payout."

I nodded, feeling like my head was going to explode with all the information being crammed inside so quickly.

"Are you okay?"

"I'm not happy that you didn't tell me sooner. This is the kind of thing that we should be handling together."

"You'd just been through so much with Romano, I didn't want to upset you with anything else."

"But that's part of us being a team. We talk things out and work out issues together. You've got to quit trying so hard to protect me that you end up alienating me."

"You're right. I'm sorry. I know that we've been through a lot, but can we try to put all this behind us and move forward? We're supposed to be getting married tomorrow and there's nothing more I want than to make you my wife. Can you forgive me?"

"I can as long as you promise to start including me in this stuff. Okay?"

"Deal." Teo smiled, took my hand, and gave it a little squeeze. "Now what do you say we go practice getting married?"

I let out a little chuckle before a sobering thought came to mind.

"There's one thing I don't understand and that we haven't really addressed."

"What's that?"

"Someone sent me that picture of you at the bar with the other woman. Someone was there watching you close enough that they had time to get their phone out, take the picture, and send it to me."

"I know. It's something that we will have to figure out but right now, we're going to be late for our own wedding rehearsal."

Teo buckled and pulled back onto the road.

CHAPTER 20

Teo

I was still reeling from the altercation with Anna when I pulled up at the parking lot near the cliff where Mia and I were supposed to say our vows.

I escorted Mia down the short path when Mira ran toward us from the direction of the overlook.

"Teo, Mia, hang on a second," she panted, sounding slightly out of breath.

"What's wrong?" I could hear the concern in Mira's voice.

"Before you go any further, just know, we will fix it."

"Mira. What is it?" Mia asked firmly.

"Something happened to the location, but we are working on getting someone here to fix it and if they can't, we will find another spot."

"Another..." Mia started before pushing past Mira and practically running the rest of the way.

"*Fuck*," I breathed out as I took in the splintered wood beams that had once made up the wedding arch, scattered on the ground alongside flower petals and crushed bouquets. Broken wooden chairs lay in shambles on either side of what was supposed to be the aisle and there were even spray-painted obscenities on the large rocks and trees nearby.

Whoever had vandalized the cliff had spared nothing.

I squeezed Mia's hand and glanced down at her. She was trying to be strong, but her eyes glistened with unshed tears and my jaw clenched.

I spotted my father standing farther in the mess talking with Luca, Alessandro, and Dario and I hurried over to them.

"What do we know?"

"Not much," my father said solemnly.

"Enzo's gone to talk to the police to see if he can find out anything."

"I doubt they're going to be much use. Something tells me that this wasn't just some random vandals."

"You think it was someone targeting you?"

"I think we have a lot of enemies and all of them have a reason to not want Mia and I to get married."

"I don't think you're far off with that," Luca added. "Come look." He motioned for me to follow him over to one of the large rocks and nodded down at it. "Look, here on the back side of it."

"A Corsican tag. But this feels too juvenile for the Corsicans," I said thoughtfully.

"Who are you thinking?"

"I'm not sure yet. Someone young, for sure, with a grudge."

"That could be a lot of people."

"But I think I may have an idea of one potential suspect."

"Who?"

"Didn't Andrea have a brother?"

"Two actually," my father added as he joined us. "The oldest abdicated as underboss. He didn't want the job, so Andrea was next in line, but he also has a younger brother."

"Andrea's death could have pushed him to lash out."

"They're hoping to postpone the wedding long enough to buy time to stop it. I wouldn't be surprised if they were the ones behind the picture someone sent to Mia."

"What picture?"

"Some woman tried to solicit me last night and Mia mysteriously got a text with a photo of the two of us. It looked bad."

"Damn. What can we do to help?"

"I'm not going to let them win. Mia and I are going to get married tomorrow."

"What about the cliff?"

"I'll see if Mira and the other girls can help with decorations, and we'll scout out a different spot for the ceremony. But keep it low key. And be careful. These little tricks are just child's play compared to what the Romanos and the Corsicans are capable of."

I approached the group of girls all surrounding Mia, and they all turned to me.

"It looks like the Corsicans are the ones to blame for this. We found some graffiti tags on the rocks over by the cliff."

"I was just telling Mia not to worry at all about any of this. Us girls are going to handle all the decorations and we will find another location for the wedding," Mira said, and I was grateful for my sister's help. I knew it would make Mia feel better.

"Good, I've already told my guys to start scouting for another spot around the Gorge where we can set up for the ceremony."

"Teo, are you sure we should be doing this here? Now? Between the photograph that was sent to me and now the vandalism, it seems like someone is determined to make sure this wedding doesn't happen."

"And we can't let them win," I said with determination while slipping my arm around Mia's waist and pulling her closer to me.

"But is that really a good reason to get married? To make sure that someone else doesn't *win*?"

"That's not why I want to marry you. Whether it's tomorrow or ten years from now, I'm still going to want to be married to you. I love you and I know you love me too. That is the reason we are getting married. I'm just done letting other people stand in the way of finally making you mine, fully and completely."

"Don't you know, I've been yours all along?"

I pulled Mia to me and kissed her firmly, pressing her soft body firmly against mine until I could feel the heat of her skin. After a long moment, I pulled away, resting my forehead against hers.

"I will marry you tomorrow, Mia. Nothing will stand in the way of that."

"Good," Mia sighed the word, seeming more relaxed than she had been.

"Look, why don't you two let us handle things here? We all know how to walk down an aisle, so we don't really need a rehearsal. We'll sort this all out while you two go enjoy yourselves. Grab some dinner and don't worry about anything." Mira's confidence was contagious and suddenly I found myself feeling as though I really didn't have anything to worry about.

"Okay. Mia? What do you say?"

Mia looked at Mira and the other's gathered around us. "If you're sure."

"Positive. Now, go, you two."

CHAPTER 21

Teo

I took Mia and left the rehearsal. My focus was on keeping her calm and not letting her give up on our wedding. I knew how important it would be to her to have a real wedding ceremony, and I would be damned if I was going to miss the opportunity to finally watch her walk down that aisle to me, knowing that she was finally going to be mine.

Mira and the other girls were determined to make sure that everything was wonderful for Mia, and I was so happy that she had friends and family in her life that were willing to go so far to ensure her happiness. My guys were working on finding the perfect location and, while I was supposed to leave it up to them, I made sure that they knew to run everything by me first.

I wanted to make sure that things were perfect, and I wouldn't leave it in anyone's hands but my own from that point on. After a romantic dinner for two in my hotel room, I dropped Mia off in her room for the night.

As much as I tried to insist on Mia staying in my room so that I could keep an eye on her, she was determined to have some tradition in the wedding which I could respect.

As soon as I arrived back at my hotel I went to work calling Mira to check on their progress.

"Yes, brother. Everything's coming together wonderfully. The guys found the perfect location. It's lower down on a secluded little spot on the water. It's beautiful and we're setting up some simple yet elegant decorations. Mia is going to love it."

"Good. Have some of the guys guard the location and shifts. I don't want any more incidents, and I'm not leaving anything else to chance."

"Will do."

"Thank you, Mira. For everything you have done for Mia—and for me."

"It's what family does, and Mia is as much my family as she will be yours soon."

"Well, in any case, thank you."

"Of course. And I'll get Luca to organize security for the new ceremony location."

"Thank you. I'm going to give Alessandro a call and get him to arrange for the guys to guard Mia's hotel room as well. I want someone watching her constantly until I can be with her."

"And what about you?"

"What about me?"

"You need someone watching out for you too."

"I don't need anyone watching out for me. I can take care of myself."

"While you sleep? And you have to sleep the night before your wedding. I think Mia would agree with me and it would help all of us to rest easier."

"Okay. Fine." I resigned with a sigh. "I'll have someone watching outside my hotel room as well."

"Good. Thank you."

That night after everything had been arranged, I sat in my hotel suite, having a drink with my father, when my phone rang.

"Hello?"

"Sir." I recognized the voice as Alessandro's man I had met earlier in the evening when he took over for the last guy to guard my room.

"Tomas, what's wrong?"

"Rocco just spotted someone suspicious outside of Mia's room. When he went to check it out, the guy ran. He's still got them on the run, but he needs backup.

"So, Mia's room is unguarded? Go help him find the guy. I'm heading to her room now to make sure that she's okay."

I hung up the phone and called out to my dad, letting him know what was going on as I grabbed my keys and ran out the door toward Mia's room. I hated that I'd let her convince me that we shouldn't be in adjoining rooms at the very least. She wanted there to be a little distance so that we didn't accidentally run into each other when she was transporting her wedding dress or leaving for the ceremony.

I finally made it to her room and tried to enter, but it was locked. I banged on the door, making it rattle until Mia quickly opened it.

"Teo? What's going on? What are you doing here?"

"Rocco spotted someone suspicious and Tomas is helping him track them down. I'm here to make sure that you're safe."

"I'm fine. I didn't even know there was anything going on. Come in."

Mia stepped aside, and I hurried inside, locking the door behind us. I checked the windows and the back door that led out to her balcony, but everything was secure.

"Teo? Teo," Mia called out to me as I cleared one room at a time. "I'm fine. No one's here."

I finally stopped and looked at her, pulling her to me, and holding her tight against my chest, just breathing in her scent and assuring myself that she was safe.

"I just need you to be safe." I let out of breath and my shoulders sagged in relief and exhaustion.

"I am safe," Mia assured me.

"I don't just mean right now. I mean in general. I worry about you all the time. I worry that something might happen to you, that you might be taken away from me when I finally found you again—when things finally worked out so that we could be together. I'm still constantly worried that something or someone is going to tear you out of my arms and out of my life. You filled a hole in my heart that I didn't know was there but now that I know what it's like to have you, there's no way I could live without you, Mia.

"I love you too." Mia smiled softly and nuzzled her cheek against my chest as I held her tight. "But I'm fine now. I'm safe and I am yours—always. Tomorrow is just a formality. A wonderful formality that I'm looking forward to but a formality nonetheless, because I'm already yours, heart and soul."

"And body." I smirked down at her with a mischievous grin, and she smiled, that familiar blush coloring her cheeks.

"And body," she confirmed.

I pulled her a little closer and kissed her lips. Her body melted into mine and I deepened the kiss.

When Mia's soft moan vibrated against my lips, I lost all control. I tangled my fingers into her hair as the kiss turned desperate and wild.

I walked Mia backward, stumbling through the suite without ever breaking the kiss until we made it into the bedroom. The back of Mia's legs hit the edge of the mattress and she fell back onto the plush bed. I stood there for a moment, allowing myself to drink her in before pouncing.

171

I practically tore Mia's clothes from her body before removing mine as well. I needed to feel her warm, soft skin against mine. I trailed desperate kisses down her body, making her moan and writhe under me but I couldn't keep it up for long. I needed her more than I needed to breathe.

I plunged inside of her in one smooth thrust and sunk all the way to the hilt. She was so ready for me, it was like gliding over silk as I pulled out and dove back in again. I slipped my arms under her, cupping my hands on her shoulders to pull her down as I thrust harder, needing to get deeper.

Mia moaned in pleasure, and I swallowed her cries with each claiming kiss until both of us came apart, jolting and jerking as we rode the waves of ecstasy. I collapsed beside Mia, pulling her naked body tight against me and kissed her gently.

I held Mia in my arms until she drifted off to sleep. The idea of leaving that bed was almost unbearable. It took every bit of willpower I had to slide out from under the sheet, get dressed, and walk out the door. But Mia was traditional, and I knew that it would mean a lot to her to at least maintain some traditions for our wedding. I jotted down a quick note before leaving and headed back to my room.

After one last round of text to everyone, making sure everything was ready for the next day, I took a shower and climbed into bed.

I practically jumped out of bed the next morning from pure excitement. I was finally going to marry Mia. After everything we had gone through and everything that had happened, it was finally all going to be worth it when

172

she became my wife. I wanted to get an early start to make sure that there was nothing wrong with the ceremony location or any of the vendors. I wanted the day to be perfect for Mia.

I called Rocco to let him know that I was almost ready to leave. I was sure that he would be relieved to go get some sleep.

"Hey boss. Everything okay?"

"Everything's good. I just wanted to let you know that I'm about ready to head to the ceremony site. Then you'll be able to go to your room and get some sleep."

"Sounds good. I will go pull your car around, then I'll be ready to crash."

"Just make sure you're out of my car before you crash," I teased, and Rocco let out a warm laugh.

"You got it boss. I don't plan on crashing until I am in my bed."

"I want to thank you for last night. If you and Tomas had not been able to apprehend that guy, Mia and I would not have rested nearly as easily. You did good work, and I won't forget it."

"Thanks, boss. I'd do anything for the family."

"You're a good man, Rocco. I'll see you soon."

I ended the call and slipped my phone into the pocket of my tux jacket before grabbing my keys and walking out the door.

I stepped outside and on to the sidewalk that lined the roundabout in front of the hotel. I could see my car from there and I felt silly standing there waiting as Rocco rushed across the parking lot to get it, but it was how things had been done for decades. If I'd tried to do it myself, it would have been like a slap to the face for him. It was a tradition I planned to change eventually, but it would take some time for people to get used to, and there were more important policies and issues that needed my attention first.

So, I stood there waiting like an invalid as one of our soldiers unlocked my car and climbed inside.

I pulled out my phone to text Mia when a loud blast shook the windows of the hotel and I ducked. A lady nearby screamed. People began running and shouting, not knowing what had happened. A ball of smoke billowed up from the parking lot and I looked out to see my car completely enveloped in flames. I ran as fast as I could toward the fire. Some of my men poured out of the hotel to join me. I reached for the driver door handle, but the heat made me snatch my hand back. I covered my face with my jacket and tried to move closer again using my sleeve but there was no use. I couldn't get close enough to the car, and by the looks of the flames, Rocco was long gone. There was nothing left to save.

A couple of my guys pulled me back and I breathed out a string of curses.

"How did this happen? Find out how this happened," I barked the orders just as Luca and Alessandro came out to join me.

"What happened?" Lucas asked.

"This was a hit," Alessandro stated the obvious, but I let it slide considering that we were all in shock.

174

"We had guards out all night. But when that one guy went after Mia, I sent my security detail to help find him. I left my room to go to Mia's to check on her. That gave them plenty of time to plant the bomb."

"*Shit,* Rocco." Luca let out a sigh and shook his head.

"He was a loyal soldier," I said with a heavy sign. "Does he have any family we need to contact?"

"No. We were his family," Alessandra said with a grave expression on his face as he stared at the flames dancing in the car. "I'll take care of this. You've got a wedding to get to."

"So do you. I need you there today."

Alessandro gave a nod. "I'll make a call and get a couple of our guys over here to take care of this mess."

"Thank you. And let's get a sweep on Mia's car and anyone else in the family. I won't lose anyone else."

"Should we call and let the girls know what's going on?"

"No. There's no reason to darken their day. Just get their cars checked. If we find anything, we get it out of there, and they never have to know."

"Okay."

"Knowing Mia, she's going to want to get an early start today. I need to delay her a little bit."

I pulled out my phone and began dialing.

"What are you going to do?" Luca asked curiously while Alessandro stepped away to make his calls.

"I'm creating a diversion."

"Room service. How may I help you?" A bright young sounding woman answered the phone, and I turned my attention to her.

"Hi. Yes I would like to order an assortment of breakfast choices from your menu for room one-sixty-four."

"Of course, sir. We have a breakfast sampler that sounds like what you're looking for. How many people will be eating?"

"Just one."

"Of course, sir."

"If I leave a note at the front desk, could you see that it is delivered along with the breakfast?"

"Yes of course, sir."

"Good. Thank you. I'll include specific instructions with the note."

"Perfect. Thank you, sir."

And with that, I ended the call. I had work to do and a wedding to prepare for.

CHAPTER 22

Mia

After a relaxing and romantic night with Teo, I felt better about the wedding. A text from Mira claiming to have everything under control helped. But considering all the sabotage we'd dealt with over the past months, I was still on edge.

I'd gone to sleep, wrapped in Teo's arms but when I woke, he was gone. Panic shot through me and worry took over. I threw the sheet off of my legs and jumped out of bed.

"Teo? Teo?" My voice rose with each moment that I didn't see him until I finally noticed a note on the bedroom door.

Mia,

I know how you feel about tradition, and I thought we could use all the luck that we could get. So, in keeping with the tradition of not seeing the bride before the wedding, I left early to check on the last-minute changes. I love you, and I can't wait to see you finally walk down the aisle to me. I ordered you room service. I know you're nervous about everything going smoothly today but make sure you eat something. The girls should arrive by ten for you all to get ready together. Enjoy every moment of your special day.

I'll be waiting for you at the altar,

Teo

I couldn't help but smile reading Teo's words. I couldn't wait to marry him. After a quick trip to the restroom, I made my way to the main room where the small dinette table was already filled with a delicious array of French breakfast foods.

I poured myself a glass of juice and dug in. Once breakfast was done, I went into the bathroom to take a shower. I was just lathering up when my stomach roiled. An overwhelming sense of nausea struck me all at once. I hopped out of the shower just in time to throw up.

I threw up two more times before I was able to climb back into the shower and rinse the soap from my body.

After my shower was done I wrapped myself in a fuzzy robe and sat on the bed. I pulled out my phone and called Mira.

"*Ciao,* Mia. Vittoria, Courtney, and I are just heading to your room."

"Okay." I nearly croaked the word through my strained throat.

"What's wrong? You don't sound good."

"It's nothing. I just feel sick."

"It's probably just your nerves."

"My nerves have been bad before. This is different. I think I might actually be sick. Unless…"

"Unless what?"

"Well, I didn't throw up until after I ate breakfast."

"Do you think the food was bad?"

"I think that nothing is a coincidence right now. We've had too many attempts to sabotage this wedding already."

"You think someone did this on purpose?" Mira sounded shocked. "I suppose food poisoning isn't a far stretch from all that they've done. We'll be right there."

"I can't let this ruin the wedding. Not just because these people are trying to stop it but because I want to be married to Teo."

"We will see what we can do for you as soon as we get there. I'm going to get room service to bring you sports drinks, water, Jell-O, and anything else I can think of that's good for stomach problems."

"I don't know if that's a good idea. The breakfast I ate was from the kitchen here."

"I will call the manager of the hotel restaurant and get him to personally oversee the preparation of everything. You just lay down and rest until we get there."

"Okay. Thank you Mira." We hung up the phone and I leaned back on the headboard and closed my eyes.

Mira already had a key to my room in case of emergency, so she let herself in when they arrived.

"Oh, you poor thing," Vittoria said quietly as she walked over and felt my forehead with the back of her hand. "You're not running a fever. I think you're right. It could be something you ate."

"I agree," Mira said. "Which is why it's important that we give you all the fluids we can to try to flush whatever it is out of your system."

Room service arrived a short time after with everything from dry toast to electrolyte drinks, and bananas.

For the next two hours, Mira and the other girls employed every known old-wives tale to help relieve me of my food poisoning and by mid-afternoon, I felt almost completely better.

We rushed out of the hotel with bags of beauty products and our dresses draped over our arms as we hurried to the car. We had to skip the massages, but Mira had been able to reschedule our hair and makeup appointments. It was nice to sit back and catch my breath, knowing that we were back on schedule.

Once we were finished with our makeovers, the four of us piled into Mira's rental car with our dresses in the trunk and headed toward the gorge.

180

"Thank you all so much for helping me feel better."

"That's what we're here for." Vittoria smiled at me and squeezed my shoulder from her seat in the back.

"We make pretty good physicians if I do say so myself." Mira playfully smirked at me from the driver seat, and I chuckled.

"I'll have to warn Arman that he might have some competition."

"Tell him I said to bring it." Mira laughed.

Another small twinge of nausea came over me and I popped a ginger candy into my mouth.

"Still feeling bad?" Mira glanced at me with concern.

"Just a little wave every now and then but I'm feeling a lot better."

"I can't believe you got food poisoning on your wedding day." Courtney added from the back.

"I can't believe I got kidnapped on my first wedding day, held captive, then had my wedding location vandalized. By this point, the food poisoning does not surprise me in the least."

"I guess you have a point there. I sort of feel like we should wrap you in bubble wrap until you say, '*I do*.'"

We all let out a chuckle but part of me didn't think that Courtney was far off with her idea. I worried that even a small wedding in a public place would be too dangerous after everything our enemies had tried to do to keep us apart.

Part of me wondered if we should have had the wedding at the compound where the security was highest.

Part way through my makeover, Teo texted me the new location for the ceremony and I'd plugged it into the GPS. He assured me that it was just as beautiful as our original location but by that point I didn't care. I just wanted to be married to him. I hadn't even told him about getting sick for fear that he would decide to postpone even though he'd been just as determined as I was.

We were about a half an hour away from the new spot at the gorge when police lights flashed in the rearview mirror.

"What the hell?" Mira checked the speed on the dash. "I wasn't speeding." She slowed the car and pulled off to the side with the police car pulling up right behind us.

I glanced back, watching as the police officer got out of his car and came to Mira's window.

"License and registration."

"Of course, officer. Can I ask why I'm being stopped?"

"Suspicious driving patterns." He kept his tone even with no afflictions, but I didn't like the way he never looked directly at Mira.

"What exactly does that mean?" I asked. "She wasn't speeding, she hasn't even changed lanes in the last five miles. I can't imagine what would be suspicious about her flawless driving."

"Only someone with something to hide drives perfectly so that they don't get pulled over."

"Well, now that's a stretch." I couldn't help the incredulousness of my tone as Mira handed him her paperwork on the rental car.

"Not a local, I take it, Ms. Venturi?"

"No. I'm an Italian citizen as you can see from my identification."

"Yes. An international driver's license. You travel a lot?"

"Enough that I've found the license helpful."

"And what do you travel for?"

"For school, for the fun of it, for visiting family...What does this line of questioning have to do with anything?"

"Do you have any drugs on you or in your vehicle?"

"Drugs? Of course not."

"I'm going to need you ladies to step out of the vehicle if you don't mind."

"Actually, we do mind. We are on the way to my friend's wedding, and we are already running late."

"Get out of the car, *Madame*."

Mira let out a frustrated huff but gave us a nod and we all climbed out of the car.

"I need you four to all place your hands on the hood of the car for me."

"I really don't like how you are treating us," Vittoria finally spoke up. "We haven't done anything to make you believe that any of this is necessary."

"Four international women in a rental car, driving suspiciously..."

"We weren't driving suspiciously," I snapped but Mira cast me a warning glance.

"I'm going to need to search this vehicle to make sure that you aren't smuggling drugs or other illegal paraphernalia."

"You do not have permission to search my vehicle."

"Why?" The officer got right up in Mira's face. "Because you've got something to hide?"

"No. Because we haven't done anything wrong, and this is harassment. You don't have probable cause to search the vehicle."

"I have probable cause because you refused to allow me to search. That leads me to suspect that you have something to hide."

"Or because it is her right to do so," I snapped, momentarily removing my hands from the car without thinking.

The policeman drew his gun from his side, causing all of us to shriek.

"I said put your hands on the car, *pute*. Now," he yelled while pointing his gun in my direction.

"Okay, okay," I was terrified of the gun pointed at me and quickly put my hands back on the car.

"You tourists have no respect for our laws. I'm taking all four of you in."

"What? No," I cried out. "It's my wedding day. Please?"

"You should have thought about that before you decided to cause trouble during this routine stop."

"Routine? You have been all over us since you pulled us over." Vittoria was angry but was careful never to take her hands from the car. We learned that the hard way.

The officer roughly grabbed Mira's wrists and tugged them behind her back, making her wince.

"You don't have to be so rough. She's not resisting," I warned.

"You, shut your mouth." He roughly tightened the zip ties around her wrists and stepped toward me.

I braced myself as he tugged my arms back behind my back, but the discomfort was nothing compared to the pain I'd endured at the hands of Andrea less than a week before. Just as he moved to cuff Courtney, another police car pulled up and an older officer climbed out.

"Looks like you've got your hands full here, Barre."

"Just apprehending these troublemakers," Officer Barre stated proudly to the approaching man.

"We weren't causing any trouble. He has no grounds to arrest us," Mira called out to the man, and he looked intrigued.

"What are the charges?"

"Refusing a search, resisting arrest..."

"No one is resisting," I called out.

"What was the reason for the stop?" the older officer asked while eying Officer Barre suspiciously.

"Suspicious driving patterns."

"What kind of suspicious patterns?"

"She was overly careful, following all the rules perfectly."

"So, you're arresting her for being *too* good of a driver?"

"Only someone with something to hide is that careful."

"We were just on the way to a wedding. She's getting married today." Courtney motioned toward me with her head, careful to remain touching the car.

"Barre, are you really going to arrest this woman and her friends...on her wedding day?"

"That's their story but I haven't seen any proof."

"My wedding dress is in the trunk. Go ahead and look."

The older officer nodded and popped the trunk to reveal our dresses. "Release these women and let them go. It's her wedding day."

"But..."

"Now." The older officer slammed the trunk shut.

Officer Barre looked furious as he released Courtney's wrists and cut Mira and my wrists free.

"You're free to go. You ladies drive safe," he grumbled.

I fought back the urge to make a snide remark and instead, chose to simply be relieved that I hadn't ended up in jail on my wedding day.

We climbed back into the car but before we could pull away, Officer Barre leaned into my window and whispered, "Domenico Romano sends his regards."

I gaped at him with wide eyes as Mira quickly pulled out onto the road again.

"What the hell? Who is Domenico Romano?" I looked to Mira for answers.

"Andrea's little brother. He's the one behind all of this. I should have known."

"*Shit*. You mean there's more of them?"

"Don Romano has three sons. Andrea was the middle."

"The middle? But I thought he was in line to be don?"

"He was. Romano's eldest son abdicated from his role as heir."

"He abdicated? Why?"

"I'm not sure. A lot of rumors floated around in regard to that, but we've never devoted much time to discovering the truth. All that mattered was that he said he wanted no part in it and took off to the US to distance himself from the family name."

"And the youngest?"

"More ruthless than his brother. Most of what I know about him are rumors too, but I guess with Andrea dead, Domenico would be next in line."

"So, we just traded one monster for another?" I sighed, feeling discouraged.

"No. We got rid of one so that we can move on to the next challenge."

"If he's so ruthless, why do all of these petty things to ruin the wedding? Not that I'm not grateful, but why not do something more sinister?"

"My guess? He's playing with you the way a cat plays with a mouse before it rips its head off."

"Well, that's a terrible analogy."

"But very true," Vittoria added. We need to be ready for anything.

"I'm starting to think this whole wedding is a bad idea. We should do things more low-key to not draw unwanted attention."

"Mia, there's always going to be some threat lurking around the corner, but you can't let it stop you from living."

CHAPTER 23

Mia

We arrived at the wedding site later than expected and I hurried from the parking lot, following Mira toward a small souvenir shop.

"Where are we going?"

"This location didn't have a place for us to change so I convinced the owner to let us use her back room as a changing room—for a fee of course."

We hurried into the cozy little boutique and a lady behind the counter perked up at the chime of the door bells.

"Ms. Venturi, welcome, welcome. This must be the bride to be." She grinned brightly at me.

190

"I am."

"Well, I am honored to have the future Mrs. Venturi use my humble shop. Please come with me. I took the liberty of clearing out some of my overstock clutter and brought a few mirrors I had laying around at home so you would have a proper place to prepare for your big day."

I glanced at Mira, surprised by the overly accommodating shopkeeper and Mira smiled sheepishly. "A rather large fee."

I laughed and shook my head before looking back at the shopkeeper. "That was very thoughtful of you, thank you."

"My pleasure."

"We better hurry. There won't be any time for pictures before the wedding, but we can get them all after." Vittoria hurried us into the back room to get dressed.

After a frantic couple of days, we were finally dressed and ready to head down to the spot the guys had found for the ceremony, set up on the edge of the deep, crystal water. As I made my way down the path, I noticed a familiar spot just off to the right of the wedding arch where the water toppled from the overhanging rock into the water below. It was the place where Teo had kissed me when we visited the gorge during that summer together.

I'd been filled with a mix of emotions, happy to be there in Teo's arms, but sad that our summer was coming to an end. I'd wanted so badly to tell him then that I was falling for him and that I wanted to see where things would go if we gave our relationship a real shot, but I'd hesitated because I was afraid of being rejected.

How right it seemed that we would be saying our vows just a few yards from that very spot. I paused as I neared the foliage that blocked me from Teo's view. Arman joined me there, offering his arm, and I took it. We waited as each groomsman escorted each bridesmaid down the aisle to the beautiful song flowing from the talented quartet and my heart leaped in my chest as the final couple found their place and the music shifted.

I moved to take my first step down the aisle when Arman gently held me back. "Wait. I almost forgot."

He quickly reached into the inside pocket of his tuxedo and pulled out the small silver picture frame that he had given me back when I thought that he would be walking me down the aisle to marry Gio. So much had changed in just a few short months. I smiled at the small photograph of my father, while Arman wrapped the attached silver chain around the base of my bouquet so that my father's charm hung just under the flowers.

"Now, he can be with you today, too."

I smiled, gently running my finger along the frame as a small reminder that it was there.

"Ready?" Arman looked down at me with a smile.

I took a deep breath and nodded. I stepped out from the greenery and into the view of Teo and all our guests who stood on either side of the sandy aisle. As my gaze met Teo's, each step grew easier as if I were propelled by some unseen force. His eyes never left mine and I found myself holding my breath at the intensity of his stare. He didn't blink, not once, until Arman kissed my cheek and passed my hand to him.

Then he smiled, the look so filled with love and admiration that it stole my breath and tears sprung to my eyes from the overwhelming love I felt for him.

We turned to face each other and Teo took my hands in his before whispering where only I could hear. "I want to say that I'm sorry that it took us so long to get here, but seeing you, standing here on the bank where I first realized that I loved you, I just can't lie to you like that."

I shook my head and smiled. "This is where we were always meant to get married. It just took us a little while to get here."

"I can honestly say it was well worth the wait."

Teo's thumb gently ran little circles over my knuckle as he gazed at me. The officiant began the ceremony, but I barely heard a word of it, my focus fully on Teo, lost in his eyes. The spell was only slightly disrupted when Nic handed Teo the rings and we placed the white gold bands on each other.

I glanced back at Teo, and his gaze softened as he mouthed the words '*I love you*' and I returned them to him.

"I now pronounce you, husband and wife. You may kiss your bride." The officiant barely got the last of the words from his mouth before Teo pounced on me, cradling the back of my head as he dipped me into a deep, passionate kiss that elicited several whoops and hollers from the small crowd. He stood me back upright and everyone applauded.

My heart swelled almost to bursting as I stood there. We'd finally managed to get married. I was his and he was mine and I couldn't have been any happier. Teo squeezed his arm around my waist, pulling me tighter against him as he lowered his lips to my ear.

"Now you're all mine."

I looked up at him, his eyes sparkling with mischief.

After some photos at the gorge, our family and friends gathered along the sides of the path back toward the cars, everyone grinning as they threw flower petals up into the air as Teo and I headed for the car. When we reached the top of the hill a long black limo waited for us.

"You got us a limo?" I looked at Teo with delight.

"You didn't think I was going to waste any time driving my bride back to the hotel did you? This way I can have you all to myself for the entire ride." Teo's eyes lit up again with a wolfish grin and my heart kicked up a few beats.

The driver opened the door and Teo escorted me inside immediately pushing the button to close the privacy screen. We would have roughly two hours before we arrived back at the hotel.

"Champaign?" Teo asked as he pulled out two glasses.

"Yes, please."

He poured us each a glass and handed one to me. I took a sip of my champagne but was quickly distracted by Teo's lips trailing hot kisses down my neck and to my shoulder. I nearly dropped my glass as my head fell to the side with a moan. Teo placed my champagne to the side while letting his lips continue their exploration, gently tugging at the neckline of my dress to get better access.

"Teo," I moaned as he reached back and unzipped my dress, allowing his mouth to descend over my breast and my back arched.

"I have two hours with you, and I don't want to waste a moment. Now take off this dress."

After nearly two hours of ecstasy, Teo and I lay tangled and breathless in the seat of the limo. We would be having a small family dinner in lieu of a big reception until we got home. There we would have the large traditional reception with family, friends, and *the family* along with a few important associates.

"As much as I hate to say this, we should probably get cleaned up and dressed before we arrive. Not that I would mind, but I'm sure that you wouldn't want our guests knowing what we've been up to."

"Mm," I hummed out an incoherent response, and Teo's chest jumped under my cheek as he laughed.

"Come on, *la mia bellissima moglie.*"

He moved, stirring me from my sedated state and began helping me clean up and dress which was challenging in the back of the limo.

I did my best to tame my mussed hair and smudged makeup before we pulled up to the hotel.

We were just stepping inside when Vittoria spotted me and hurried over. "I'd ask what took you two so long, but I think your hair and makeup says it all." She chuckled.

I self-consciously ran my fingers over my hair. "Is it that bad?"

"It won't be when I get done with it. Come with me."

I flashed Teo a smile as Vittoria pulled me toward the women's bathroom.

A few stray strands of hair re-secured and makeup touched up and I was ready to join the party. I stepped outside of the bathroom and into the foyer where Teo stood, talking intensely to Enzo.

He stopped and smiled at me as I approached. "Better, now?"

I nodded. "I'm not interrupting anything am I?"

"Of course not." Teo wrapped his arm around my waist, pulling me to his side.

"I was just congratulating our don," Enzo said smoothly but he was lying.

If that was a congratulatory conversation, it was the most intense one I'd ever witnessed. I wouldn't call him out on it, though. Not when he was clearly taking his cues from my husband.

"We shouldn't keep everyone waiting," Teo squeezed my hip slightly and nodded to Enzo before pulling me away.

Once we were out of earshot, I glanced up at him while otherwise not changing my expression. "So, are you going to tell me what that was really about?"

"What?"

"That extremely intense congratulations that Enzo was offering to you."

I looked at him with a skeptically raised eyebrow and he smiled affectionately at me.

"You caught on to that, huh?"

"I'm very observant, but it wouldn't have taken my impressive observation skills to know that it was more than a casual conversation."

"Some of my men remained in Corsica when we left. They're doing some recon. I needed to have eyes there. And they've picked up on some chatter that may hopefully lead to the men responsible for the attacks in Nice and the ones on us now. There's nothing definitive, which is why I wasn't going to say anything to you until I knew more. I don't want this overshadowing our wedding day."

"That's all I needed to know. Thank you for telling me. Although, I hope we can get to the point where you come tell me without me having to catch you."

"Now what would the fun in that be?" Teo smirked playfully and pulled me a little closer to his side.

We came to a stop just outside the private dining hall where our family waited. He turned to look at me, lifting my chin with a crooked finger so that my eyes met his. "I promise, I will be open and honest with you about my business dealings. I don't want us hiding anything from each other anymore. I want us to be a team. Like you said."

"Good. Because I think we make a pretty spectacular one."

"As do I. Now, wife, I think it's time we enjoy our celebration. God knows it's been a long time coming."

CHAPTER 24

Teo

The day after our wedding, we flew home, and the very next evening, was our wedding reception where we planned to make our official debut in front of all the members of the family. It would be the first time our two families were in the same place at the same time on such a large scale.

Mia's hand trembled in mine. We wanted peace between our families and the reception to be a happy occasion for all. Because even after only two days, I already knew that I was going to be happy with Mia as my wife.

We walked into the elegant reception hall decorated in cream and gold. And everyone began applauding as we entered. The musicians quit playing and the man near the microphone began speaking.

"Ladies and gentlemen, may I introduce to you for the first time, Mr. and Mrs. Matteo Venturi."

Everyone cheered. And Mia grinned from ear to ear. I squeezed her hand and led her into the middle of the dance floor just as the band began playing a romantic, slow song. I tugged Mia into my arms, resting one hand on the small of her back, gently pressing her soft, warm body against mine while my other hand cradled her hand.

I led Mia in a traditional waltz, and she smirked up at me. "I didn't know that you could dance like this."

I spun her out and back to me, making her smile. "I'm a man of many secrets and many talents."

"Not *too* many. I hope," Mia teased with a sparkle in her eye.

"Just enough to keep my wife from getting bored."

"Oh, trust me, I don't see myself getting bored with you anytime soon."

"Oh, but you do see it happening eventually?" I raised an eyebrow and smirked.

"When we are old and gray, with grandchildren running around the house, I believe you will still be keeping me on my toes," she laughed.

"Grandchildren? We'd have to have children before we could have that."

"That's true."

"I suppose we should get started then." I wagged my eyebrows at her, and her eyes widened.

"Started?"

"Well, at least we can start practicing for when we are ready to start a family."

"That's something we never really talked about...starting a family."

"And it's something we *will* talk about. When the time is right." Mia didn't seem ready for that conversation. I guessed that our wedding reception wasn't the time or place to discuss starting a family. Besides, there would be plenty of time for that.

Once the song was done, I led Mia to our table where our wedding meal would be served.

After our meal, Mia and I stood together, watching our guests take to the dance floor while others came by to wish us well. As one of Enzo's men moved on, I looked out at the ballroom, filled with my family and Mia's mingling together and I felt hope for a future filled with peace instead of feuds and danger.

Vittoria stood by the bar, chatting with Enzo and a few other people while Courtney danced with one of my men.

"Do you think there's something between them?" Mia inclined her head toward the opposite side of the dance floor, and I tried to follow her gaze.

"Who?"

"Mira and Luca."

I scoffed and held back a laugh at the absurdity. "Mira? And Luca? How much champagne have you had?"

"What? Why is that so ridiculous? I see them together a lot. They seem close."

"Luca is like my brother. I've known him my whole life. Mira too. That's all you're seeing."

"Are you sure? I just think—"

"I'm sure," I assured her before another group of guests came to offer their congratulations.

As one of my men moved away, I spotted a familiar guest approaching. Senator Ricci smiled and shook my hand before moving on to Mia. He seemed eager to speak with her which made me curious, so I did my best to focus on their conversation while filtering out the small talk of other guests coming by to shake my hand.

"Ms. Monticelli, or should I say Mrs. Venturi now?" The senator smiled and offered Mia his hand.

"Mia, please? And I am so glad that you were able to join us, Senator."

"I wouldn't have missed it. You look lovely as always, Mia. Marriage agrees with you."

As they exchanged pleasantries I was suddenly pulled from their conversation when Alessandro took me by the arm.

"Teo, I need to speak with you for a moment."

"Can't it wait?"

"I'm afraid not."

I gave him a nod, and we found a quiet corner where we could talk.

"Alright, what's going on?"

Alessandro leaned in to whisper conspiratorially. "One of my men who stayed behind in Corsica just called me. He found where Graziani has been hiding."

"Shit, that's fantastic news." As the Corsican's leader, finding Graziani would go a long way toward taking down their organization once and for all.

"I'd like your permission to take a couple of teams down there so that we can take him out once and for all."

"I don't know, Alex. It's a dangerous mission. You're supposed to be my underboss now that I'm taking over as don."

"As your underboss, and your friend, let me do this for you and Mia. Let me give you the wedding present of peace by eliminating one of your biggest threats."

"Call La Guerriglia to join you with his men and take Luca and a team of his men with you, too. I want others down there to have your back."

"Thank you." Alessandro moved to leave but I called after him. "Hey, Alex…"

"Yeah?"

"Take that bastard down."

"Yes, sir." Alessandro gave me a determined nod before grabbing Luca and heading for the door.

As soon as Alessandro was gone, Mia headed by direction. "*Ciao*, my love."

"*Ciao, bellissima.* Are you enjoying the celebration?" I placed my arm around her waist and pulled her against me. I wasn't sure what it was about her, but I craved her body against mine all the time.

"Yes. It's wonderful. But what was that before with Alessandro? Is everything all right?"

"Everything's fine. I was just waiting until you were done talking to the senator to come talk to you. One of the men we left behind in Corsica was able to locate the men who were responsible for the attack in Nice as well as helping Romano with kidnapping and holding you. I'm sending Alessandro and Luca down with some of their men to hunt them down and take them out once and for all."

"Just them? Will that be enough to take them down?"

"La Guerriglia and some of his men will also be meeting them there to offer support. Then this will be done, once and for all."

"I can't even imagine what that would be like. No longer having to worry or look over our shoulders all the time."

"We will always have to be vigilant. With the power we hold, there will always be enemies, but it would alleviate a large portion of our concern. I may even be able to start working from the office more often, instead of staying home to keep an eye on you."

"Oh, well, maybe we need to rethink this then because I like having you at home," Mia teased though I suspected it was partially true.

"Yes, but then I'd get to leave more of my work at work, and I'd get to enjoy coming home, throwing you over my shoulder and hauling you up to our bedroom every evening."

"I do like the sound of that." Mia's cheeks turned pink. She leaned in, pressing her body against mine and I lowered my lips to kiss her.

"Sir?" Alessandro interrupted apologetically and I straightened just before my lips had the chance to meet Mia's. "I'm sorry to talk business during your wedding celebration."

"It's okay. This is important."

"Did you talk to Luca?" I asked Alessandro and he nodded.

"He was just about to go gather his men."

"Good. And La Guerriglia?"

"He's all set."

"Perfect."

"Please be careful," Mia said to my surprise.

"We will be. Just think of this as a small wedding present for you both. A bit of closure after those assholes attacked in Nice."

"It will be much more than a *small* gift. I assure you." Mia gave him a genuine smile of gratitude.

"We should get going. Enjoy your honeymoon and we will see you when you get back."

"Thank you again, Alessandro."

Alessandro seemed slightly uncomfortable accepting Mia's gratitude, probably because to him, he's only doing what has to be done for the family. He never did anything for the praise which was one of the reasons I felt he would make a good underboss. He gave Mia and I a brief nod and hurried off to collect his men.

Mia let out a quiet sigh and I looked down at her. "What is it?"

"Do you really think they're going to be safe?"

"I do." I wrapped my arms around her waist and pulled her close. "We live in a dangerous world and sometimes we have to do dangerous things, but Alessandro and the other men are good at what they do. I always try my best to find where someone excels and place them in a position to succeed. There are always challenges but if they are truly where they are supposed to be then they will rise to them."

There was a sparkle in Mia's eyes and her plump, sexy lips curled up into a mischievous grin. "And what do you see that I excel at?"

"Oh, there are many positions that I know you will excel at, and I plan to test each and every one of them out while we're on our honeymoon."

"You promise?" She nearly purred as she looked up at me with a playful smirk.

I gripped her chin, tilting her head back before claiming her lips. I only pulled away enough to mutter my words against her lips. "Oh, I guarantee it."

CHAPTER 25

Mia

After another amazing night with Teo, I fell asleep in his arms, wondering if I'd even have the ability to climb out of bed in the morning.

We had put off going on our honeymoon until after our reception. I had plans for lunch with the girls but after that we would be taking the private jet to Paris for a week.

Teo wanted to take me on a month-long honeymoon around Europe. But with Nic and Mira returning to Las Vegas and Alessandro and Luca in Corsica, that only left Enzo and Dario to assist Piero in running two merging families while we were away. So, we decided that it would be better not to be gone for too long.

It had been my intention to sleep in until I had to get up to start getting ready for lunch. Since getting married, Teo had become wonderfully insatiable, and I loved every minute of it even if it left me exceedingly tired and in constant need of mid-day naps just to keep up. I stirred slightly, turning onto my back, when an intense wave of nausea struck.

I ran into the bathroom just in time to heave into the toilet. It had been a few days since my bout of food poisoning, and I worried why I might still have problems three days later. I splashed cool water on my face and walked back into the bedroom. Teo still slept soundly.

I grabbed my phone from the nightstand when another wave hit. I ran back into the bathroom but managed not to throw up again. I lowered myself into the floor, leaning against the tub in case the nausea got too bad.

I pulled out my phone and dialed Arman.

"Mia? Is everything okay?"

"Yeah. Well, sort of. I'm sorry. Did I wake you?"

"No. I'm at the clinic today. What's going on, Mia?"

"The day of the wedding, I got food poisoning after eating breakfast from the hotel."

"Food poisoning? Why didn't you call me?"

"I was just so focused on feeling well enough to go through with the wedding. And I didn't want Teo finding out and worrying. The girls helped, though."

"Okay, but you seemed okay at the wedding. What's going on now?"

"I woke up sick again today and I wanted to know if that could happen. Can you have a relapse from food poisoning?"

"It's possible but usually once you recover that's it. Why don't you come by the clinic today and let me check you out before you go on your honeymoon. You don't need to travel if you're sick."

"I'm supposed to have lunch with the girls at one and I don't even know how I'm going to be around food."

"I'm sure Vittoria and the others would understand if you don't feel up to lunch."

"I really don't want to miss it. It's the last time we will all be together until Mira's graduation in the spring."

"Okay, you could be dehydrated. That can cause nausea after being ill. If that's all it is, I can give you an electrolyte IV which should do the trick, but I'd really feel better if you'd let me check you out."

"Okay," I sighed reluctantly.

"Usually by ten, the morning rush has cleared. That would give you time to get ready for your lunch, you can run by here, I'll check you out, and if everything is okay, you can still have your time with the girls."

"Thank you, Arman. I don't know what I'd do without you."

"That's what family's for."

"Well, thank you, all the same. I'll see you soon."

We ended the call and I slowly pulled myself up off the floor and into the shower. Roughly thirty-minutes later I was slipping out the door, trying not to wake Teo. I didn't want him to worry.

I still felt nauseated as I drove to the clinic and was relieved when I arrived, to see that Arman was right about the clinic being slow.

"Mia, hi," a sweet older nurse but I vaguely remembered said in a cheerful tone. How are you?"

"I'm—"

"Oh, I suppose that's a silly question isn't it? If you were feeling well then you wouldn't be here. I'll let Dr. Monticelli know that you're here."

"Thank you." I smiled through the sick feeling that gnawed at my stomach. She disappeared behind double doors and soon after, her and Arman appeared.

"Mia," Arman said as he approached and hugged me gently. "You look pale."

"I feel worse than I look," I admitted.

"Let's get you to the back and run some tests. We'll find out what's going on."

"Thank you." I followed him through the double doors and down a long hallway that had several exam rooms on either side, along with one marked for x-rays.

Arman had plenty of family money and no need to work but he loved his job at the clinic, so much so that when funding for it suffered, he bought it as a private practice, keeping it free for those in need. He also equipped it with all the latest, state of the art equipment because he said that it wasn't fair for underprivileged people to be forced to sacrifice their health care.

My father and his both helped fund the project because it worked well for the family too. We had a legitimate doctor who kept all our secrets and a state-of-the-art facility to treat our family off the record. There was more security in the clinic than in most because my father had stocked it with Monticelli men to help keep away any enemies who might try to attack where we're weak.

Arman led me to a private room and helped me up onto the exam table. After a quick check of my vitals, he called in a nurse with a tray of syringes and vials.

"I'm just going to take a little blood so that I can run a few tests to make sure that everything's good. You're not running a fever so that's a good sign, but it also rules out most of the obvious possibilities."

"So, you don't think it's food poisoning?" I asked curiously and turned my head as he began prepping my arm.

"It's possible but the chances of it being from the breakfast you ate that morning is slim. It doesn't usually happen that fast. Most likely it would have been from something you ate the day before or even a couple of days before. The chances of it going away then coming back again is also strange. Most things hit hard and once it's out of your system it's out of your system."

"What could it be then?"

"We'll know more after these tests come back."

"I really appreciate you fitting me in so quickly. I'm sorry I didn't tell you sooner."

"It's no trouble at all. It's what I'm here for. I'm always here for you, Mia." He pulled the needle from my arm, quickly placing a small cotton ball in the crease of my arm and folding my arm to hold it in place. "I'll put a rush on this. I know you have places to go."

"Thank you."

"Of course. I'm just going to go check on one of my other patients while we wait on this, and I'll be right back. Can I have one of the nurses bring you anything? Would you like a ginger ale? It could help settle your stomach."

"I'll try anything."

"In that case I'll also have her bring you a few crackers from the break room."

Arman stepped out of the room and a few minutes later there was a quiet tapping on the door. Come in. The door slowly opened to reveal a pretty, young nurse with long straight brunette hair pulled back in a high ponytail.

"Hi. I'm Chiara. Dr. Monticelli said that you needed something to help your stomach."

"*Ciao,* Chiara. Yes, thank you."

She offered me a can of ginger ale and a pack of saltine crackers. I took them gratefully, opening the can and taking a sip.

"I also brought a few peppermint candies. I kept them around the office when I was pregnant last year and some of the kids that come in really enjoyed them, so I started keeping them all the time."

"Thank you so much. I really appreciate it. I don't know what I got into, but I feel horrible."

"I'm sure whatever it is Dr. Monticelli will be able to help. He's amazing."

"Yes he is."

"Is there anything else I can get you before I go?"

"No thank you. This is great."

"All right. Feel better soon." And with that she slipped out of the room. After a couple of crackers, the nausea seemed to dwindle and after a few more, it was nearly gone. By the time Arman came back into the room, I felt almost back to normal.

"Hey. How are you feeling?"

"A lot better, actually. The ginger ale and crackers really seem to do the trick."

"Good. I'm glad." Arman shut the door and came closer. "Well," he hesitated. "I have some good news and some news I'm not sure about yet."

"Okay let's start with the good news, then.".

"The good news is that you don't have food poisoning, a parasite, or stomach virus."

"Is it an ulcer? I just don't know what would cause all this, but I have been under a whole lot of stress lately."

"It's not an ulcer."

"Then what is it?"

"Mia, you're pregnant." Arman's words echoed in my head for a moment as I tried to process what he was saying. I wasn't sick. I was pregnant.

"*Pregnant?* Are you sure?"

"I'm pretty sure."

"That's crazy. I can't be pregnant."

"Have you had unprotected sex in the last couple of months?"

"Well, yeah but not often. We usually use protection."

"Contraception is only as effective as the person taking it or using it. If you don't use it then it can't work."

"Pregnant…" I repeated the word as I let it sink in and let the true meaning of what he was saying register. I was going to have a baby. Teo and I were going to have a baby. I remembered how upset he had been when he thought that Anna was pregnant with his child. He had been relieved that it wasn't his.

How will he feel when this one is? The nausea returned, that time from nerves more than from anything else.

"Mia? Are you okay? You're looking a little pale.

"I feel a little faint."

"Here lie back." Arman rushed over and helped lie me on the exam table before hurrying to the sink and wetting a couple of paper towels to put on my forehead.

Once I started to feel a little better, he helped me back up. "So, I take it this isn't good news? I thought you always wanted children." Arman sat on the side of the exam table and took my hand in his in a show of support.

"I did—I do. I'm just not sure that Teo does."

"Why wouldn't he?

"Something came up not so long ago that gave me a pretty good idea at how he would react if he found out I was pregnant "

"I see. Well, the fact is that you *are* pregnant. So, I guess the only thing to do now is to talk to him about it."

"I can't. Not right now. We're about to leave on our honeymoon. I can't bear to ruin that for us. Besides, if he doesn't take it well, I may need some space, and I won't be able to do that alone with him in Paris."

"You have to do what you think is best but from what I've seen, it's always better to get things out in the open instead of holding them in."

"I'm going to tell him. It's not really something I can keep secret for too long."

"That's true."

"I'm just scared. Things are so good between us, and we've been through so much. I just want a little time to enjoy being with him without all the problems we have had to face."

"Well, whatever happens, always know I'm here for you."

"I know you are. Thank you. "

"Would you like to do an ultrasound to see how far along you are?"

"I shouldn't. That feels like something Teo should be here for. It wouldn't feel right without him."

"Okay, but you need to tell him soon. And you need to see an obstetrician sooner rather than later to make sure that your baby gets the best start in life that it can."

Your baby. The words echoed in my head. I was having a baby.

"I will. Just as soon as we get back from our honeymoon."

"Okay, until then I'm going to write you a prescription for prenatal vitamins. Keep using the peppermints, ginger ale, and crackers for the nausea. You can also try ginger, but if that doesn't work, I can call you in something to help."

"I really appreciate this."

"Anything for you. And tell Chiara to give you a bag of those peppermints. That should get you through until you can pick up some before your trip."

"I will. I should go before I'm late for the girls' lunch."

"Call me if you have any questions or any problems come up. And I'll put together a recommendation for the best obstetricians in our area."

I kissed Arman on both cheeks before heading out to lunch.

CHAPTER 26

I woke up expecting to see Mia lying next to me, but her side of the bed was empty. There was no sign of her in the bathroom, or anywhere else for that matter. I checked her old room, but she wasn't there either, so I headed downstairs.

"*Buongiorno*, Bianca, Lucia. Is Mia around?"

"I haven't seen her," Lucia responded and looked at Bianca.

"I've been in the kitchen all morning, and she hasn't come in for coffee or breakfast."

"Huh, that's not like her. I'll check her office, then give her a call."

I left the kitchen and went to my old office. Mia and I were still in the process of moving things around to make it feel more like her own space. I thought she might have not been able to sleep and gone in there to work but she was nowhere to be found.

I pulled out my phone and dialed her number but there was no answer. So, I sent her a text.

Teo: Woke up without you in my arms. Where are you?

It was several minutes before I finally received an answer.

Mia: I had a couple of last-minute errands to run before my lunch with the girls. Don't worry, you'll have plenty of time with me on our honeymoon.

Teo: Never enough.

Mia: (Kiss mark emoji)

See you soon.

I caught myself smiling with a big goofy grin that I was glad the guys weren't there to see. With that mystery solved, I headed back into the kitchen for breakfast. I had a few things to wrap up for work before my official honeymoon started, so I went into my new office. My father had insisted I go ahead and move everything so that as soon as I was back, I'd be ready to take over as don. I was surprised at how eager he seemed to elevate me to don, much more so than he'd ever seemed about Gio taking on the role.

As I lowered myself into the large, leather office chair that sat behind the impressive mahogany desk, I took a moment to appreciate what that symbolized. Once I came back from my trip with Mia, I would return as don of the entire Venturi family as well as the Monticellis. It was a massive responsibility that I wouldn't take lightly. I was grateful that I had someone so intelligent, caring, and capable to stand beside me in leading our families.

I took one last deep breath before booting up my computer, but before I could dive into my work, there was a knock on the door.

"*Entrare.*"

The door opened slowly, and Dario peeked in. "*Ciao*, boss. You got a minute?"

"Of course. Come."

"*Grazie.*" Dario looked nervous as he walked inside and closed the door.

"Please, sit. What's going on?"

"I was hoping to discuss something with you before your trip, but I've struggled to find the right time."

"Well, now seems like as good of a time as any, especially since I leave tonight. What's going on?"

"I'm not sure if you've talked to Nic. I asked him to let me talk to you myself. I felt like I owed you that."

"Talk to me about what?" My shoulders tensed as my curiosity turned to concern. It wasn't often that Dario was so serious.

"You know that I value you as don. I know that you are going to do great things for our family."

"Why do I feel like there is a but coming? Let's just get to it, Dario."

"I'd like your permission to go with Nic to Las Vegas and work for him there."

"In Las Vegas?"

He nodded. "Nic said that he was having a hard time finding a good second who he can really trust. He said he couldn't think of anyone better than family, *blood*. And after how I've been doing at Gio's club, I'd like to give this a shot."

"This is what you really want?"

Dario's definitive nod told me everything I needed to know. He didn't have any doubts about moving to Las Vegas or with helping Nic run the casino. It would be good for Nic to have family there to watch his back and Dario had done a really good job with Gio's old club.

"Okay, I suggest you get packing. Nic and Mira plan to head back to the states as soon as the jet returns from dropping Mia and me off on our honeymoon."

"Really? You're sure you're good with this? I don't want any bad blood between us. I respect the hell out of you, and I want to make you proud. I want to be the kind of man who brings value to the family, not takes away from it."

"You keep saying stuff like that and I may not want to let you go," I teased.

"Okay, well in that case, I will just say *grazie* and leave it at that."

221

"*Prego*. Now, come here." I stood and Dario and I embraced as brothers before I sent him on his way. I'd have to find someone else to run the club and I would miss my cousin greatly, but the smile on his face as he turned to leave, told me that I'd made the right decision.

Once Dario left my office, I decided to give Alessandro a call before diving into my regular work.

"*Ciao*, boss."

"*Ciao*. I was just calling for a status report."

"We arrived in Corsica undetected and have settled into the safe house."

There was some hesitation in his voice that gave me an uneasy feeling. "But?" I asked expectantly.

"But we've got a small hang up with my informant. We were supposed to meet so he could give us the location of the Corsican men, but he never showed. I got a text from him afterward, saying that there were some suspicions, and he couldn't risk meeting yet. I haven't had verbal or visual confirmation from him. Only the text."

"So, it could really be anyone?" I said with a sigh.

"Unfortunately."

"Be careful. I don't like the sound of this, and it could all end up being a setup."

"We're being careful, taking every precaution we can, but boss, I want to get this guy for you and for Mia. They almost killed you five years ago and that can't stand. If you ask me they've been on borrowed time for years and it's time for us to collect."

222

The determination in Alessandro's voice at avenging my near death was touching. I was happy to have friends, capos, who care so much about the man who will be there don even when I was never truly supposed to be.

"I'm going to arrange another meeting tonight but we're going to arrive early, scout the place out, and have a few snipers around the perimeter. That way we'll be prepared for any surprises and may even lure out our enemies if it is a trap."

"I don't like the idea of you doing that. It's too risky."

"We've run this kind of thing plenty of times before."

"It's harder when you're the one calling the shots," I admitted. "More responsibility. More lives in my hands."

"I know. But we've got this."

"Okay. Just be smart about it."

"Aren't I always?"

"Most of the time." I chuckled.

"I'll check in tonight and let you know how things went. That is unless you're going to be too busy on your honeymoon." I heard the teasing tone and his voice and smiled.

"Oh, I plan to be extremely busy for the entire week of the honeymoon. But you can call. Mia understands how important this mission is. Besides, if I'm in the middle of something, I'll just call you back." I chuckled.

Alessandro laughed. "I see where your priorities lie, boss."

We ended the call, and I dove into my work for the rest of the morning. I worked through lunch, having Bianca bring me something to eat at my desk.

By midafternoon I wrapped up a conference call with some of our suppliers and closed my laptop for the day. I went upstairs to finish packing and make sure that we had everything that we would need for our trip, knowing that Mia should be home anytime for us to head to the airport.

I couldn't wait for a week away with her. I just wished that Alessandro and Luca hadn't had to take off to Corsica right as we were leaving. I would have preferred not to have been so distracted with their safety and the mission they were on so that I could devote my entire attention and all my energy on Mia. Then again, I wasn't sure that she could handle that much of my focus. What I felt for her was so intense that sometimes I feared that I might end up chasing her away.

Part of me wanted to lock her up to keep her safe and all to myself but I couldn't do that. Mia was a strong woman, smart, intelligent, and driven. Those were all the things that I loved about her, but they were also the things that made protecting her all the more challenging. I realized early on that I couldn't keep her locked away. It only caused her to put herself in more danger and created conflict between us.

I was carrying both of our suitcases down the stairs when Mia walked through the door. She didn't look quite herself. Her skin was more pale than usual, her eyes were a bit heavier, and I worry that something might be

224

wrong. I jogged down the stairs and dropped the suitcases at my feet.

"Is something wrong, *Bellissima*?"

"No, of course not." Mia smiled at me, but it was weaker than usual.

"Are you sure? You don't seem like everything's okay. You don't look like an excited bride ready to go on her honeymoon."

"I'm just tired. Someone kept me awake all night and I had to leave early for my errands and lunch with the girls."

Tired. Of course, she was tired. I'd kept her up until the sun was already starting to peek over the horizon. "I'm sorry, my love. I promise I'll make sure that you get at least a little bit of sleep on this trip." I smirked at her and pulled her close, gently tipping her chin up so that my lips could find hers. "I've already brought your suitcase and toiletry bag down, along with mine. Is there anything else that you needed?"

"No. I believe that's all."

"Good. Then I thought we should have an afternoon snack on the patio before we leave."

"That sounds nice."

I led Mia out to the patio where Bianca and Lucia were finishing preparing an antipasto spread along with Mia's favorite wine as a special treat before our flight.

"This looks wonderful. Thank you so much." I pulled out Mia's chair and she took a seat before I found mine.

"I had them bring some of your favorite wine from the vineyard." Mia looked hesitant at the bottle and smiled.

Something was definitely off but I couldn't place it and I hated not being able to figure out what was going on, but I hated it more that she wasn't confiding in me. "Do you not like this one anymore?"

"I do. It's just with being so tired I'm afraid if I have any wine, I may not be able to stay awake through the flight.

"You can always nap on the plane. It's one of the benefits of a private jet."

"I know, but I don't want to miss a moment of this honeymoon with you, not even the flight over."

"Okay. We will stick with water tonight."

"Thank you. But please, you can have some wine if you want."

"We will save this bottle for later." I smiled at her while studying her expression, trying to figure out what exactly was going on with her.

We ate our antipasto, but I was concerned. Mia lacked her usual appetite, and she was quieter than usual.

"Will you excuse me for a moment? I need to use the *bagno*."

"Of course."

I excused myself, walking into the house and immediately called Armando. I figured that if I was going to ask a question about Mia, he would be the one to ask. He answered after the third ring.

"Hello?"

"Armando, it's Matteo."

"Matteo, it's good to hear from you. Is everything all right? Is Mia okay?"

"I don't know. She's not acting right. She's pale and looks extremely tired."

"Have you asked her how she's feeling?"

"She said she's fine, but something seems off."

"Mia has been through a lot in the past few months. Everything from losing her father to being kidnapped twice. We still don't know the full extent of what Romano did to her during the time he had her in Corsica. She's going to take some time to heal emotionally and physically from everything that she's been through. I'm sure that's all it is but you should talk to her. Be patient with her. I'm sure Mia will open up to you if you make her feel safe."

"Make her feel safe? Mia *is* safe with me. I would protect her with my life," I said with some defensiveness in my tone.

"I know that and I'm sure she knows that too but sometimes a woman might need to be reminded that you're not going anywhere. That, no matter what she does, no matter what happens, she has you and your support."

I felt like Armando might know more than he was letting on. I wondered if Mia had talked to him, but I doubted that he would tell me if she had. So, I took his advice to heart, knowing that he might have some inside information he wasn't willing to share outright.

"Thank you Armando. I will do my best to do just that."

"Good. Call me if anything else comes up with Mia. I'm always happy to help. And I hope you guys have a very enjoyable honeymoon."

"Grazie." I ended the call and pocketed my phone before heading back out to Mia.

She fiddled with the food on her plate, looking wistfully into the yard when I approached. She turned to look at me with a weak smile and my heart ached for her.

"Are you about ready to head out?"

"Yes. I can't wait for this trip. I've been looking forward to an entire uninterrupted week along with you for quite some time," Mia said with a more genuine smile.

"As have I," I said with a playfully lascivious tone and Mia giggled.

CHAPTER 27

Mia

A soft kiss on my temple, followed by a gentle nudge, pulled me from a dreamless sleep. I awoke to Teo looking down at me, affectionately. As my vision came into focus, so did the interior of the plane behind him.

"I'm sorry to wake you, *bellissima*, but we're about to land."

"I slept the whole flight? I make a horrible travel companion." I groaned. I straightened in my chair and covered a yawn before buckling my safety belt.

"You must have been exhausted. I'm glad that you got some rest." Teo's gentle smile warmed my insides and made my stomach flutter.

"I'm so excited for a full week in Paris." I grinned at Teo, feeling better after my nap.

"Me too." Teo reached over and brushed a stray strand of hair from my face, tipping my head up, and pressed his lips to mine. When he pulled away, there was a look of awe in his eyes. "My beautiful wife."

I smiled at him and leaned in for another kiss when we were interrupted by the pilot over the speaker system. "Sir, there's a problem with the landing gear. We are going to have to do a belly landing. This is going to be bumpy, so I need you to brace for impact and make sure that seatbelts are secure. We touch down in one minute."

Teo straightened in his seat and adrenaline shot through my veins, causing my ears to roar and my heart to slam against the inside of my chest. I looked at him, pleading for some kind of comfort. "Teo?"

He gripped my hand tight. "Everything is going to be okay. We're going to be fine. It's just going to be a little bumpy for a few minutes."

I held my breath, waiting for impact. I squeezed Teo's hand so tight that my knuckles turned, but I couldn't bring myself to let go. Seconds ticked by excruciatingly slow as we waited for the moment when we would bounce across the runway like a skipping stone across a still pond.

The plane jolted with an awful sound of scraping and screeching metal, coming and going in rhythm with each lowering bounce.

We were thrown around like rag dolls and I was grateful for the safety belt holding me to the chair until we finally jerked to a stop with one last long screech.

I panted, roughly sucking in the needed air.

"Are you okay? Are you hurt?" Teo unbuckled his seat belt and started searching my body for any sign of injury.

"I'm fine. I'm good. I just...I'm going to be sick."

I ran to the bathroom at the back of the plane, its door haphazardly hanging open. I didn't even get to secure it as I practically dove toward the toilet before throwing up.

Teo was right behind me, and he rushed into the bathroom just in time to catch me vomiting into the toilet for the second time.

"Mia? What's wrong? Are you okay?"

"I'm fine," I said through the heaving.

"You're not fine. What's wrong? Did something happen?"

"I'm fine." I gagged again but nothing came up. "Really, I'm fine."

"We need to get you off this plane. Get you checked out. Are you okay to walk?"

"Yes. I'm good."

Teo offered me a hand and helped pull me up off the floor. I rinsed my mouth and splashed cold water on my face before letting him lead me from the bathroom to the emergency hatch and the inflatable slide which had been deployed even though the jet seemed in relatively good shape, all things considered. Emergency responders pulled up on the tarmac as we made our way from the plane and the pilot and attendants joined us.

Teo arm tightened around me, supporting me on my weak, shaking legs as he hurried me over to the ambulance.

"I need to get her checked out."

"Of course, sir. We're going to check each one of you to make sure that you are okay after that emergency landing. Does she have visible injuries?" The EMT asked.

"No, but she began vomiting right after we landed."

"It could be motion sickness from the bumpy landing, or it could be a concussion. Did she hit her head during the landing?"

"I don't think so, but everything happened so fast. We were jostled around a lot. Did you hit your head?" Teo finally asked me, and I shook my head.

"No, I didn't hit my head."

"Here, look this way for me." The EMT shined a flashlight in my eyes one at a time as he studied them. He had me follow his finger and a bunch of other silly steps there were unnecessary but I let him do his job. "Everything appears to be fine." He finally announced.

"Everything is not fine," Teo said angrily. "She threw up. Throwing up is not normal."

"No," the EMT said calmly. "But throwing up after such a rough landing could be normal the same way a person might throw up after being on a roller coaster. It's a natural response."

"Do you know who I am? I want her checked out thoroughly."

"Of course, sir. We can take her to the emergency room and let them check her out to make sure there's nothing that we are unable to assess in the field. They can do a CT or an MRI."

"Good. Then we'll do that."

"No. We won't," I said firmly, knowing that I was going to have to tell Teo about the baby a lot earlier than I had hoped.

"What do you mean we won't? You need to go to the hospital and get checked out. You were throwing up."

"I was throwing up this morning, too."

"You're sick? Why wouldn't you tell me that? We could have postponed the honeymoon for a little while until you were better."

"I'm not sick."

"I don't understand. Why didn't you tell me? Whatever is going on we could have just waited a little while until you were feeling better."

We would have been waiting quite a while. Nine months to be exact."

"Nine months?" Teo looked confused. I nodded.

After a moment, I could see the light bulb click on in Teo's eyes as they widened with realization. "Nine months? You mean…"

I nodded hesitantly. "I'm pregnant."

A strange chuckle bubbled out of Teo's chest, and he grinned at me before looking concerned.

"Why didn't you tell me? How long have you known?"

"I just found out today." I continued to explain everything that happened from the morning of our wedding to finding out about the pregnancy. My words came out hesitantly. I braced myself for the worst, unsure of how he was going to react.

"Why don't you seem more excited about this? We're going to have a baby," Teo said with excitement. His hand slipped to my lower belly, but there was no evidence of the baby yet. "Don't you want to have children?"

"Of course, I do. I just… after how you reacted to the thought of Anna being pregnant with your child, I didn't want to make you feel the same way. I didn't want you to feel stuck or obligated."

"You're my wife. I want to have children with you."

"You do?"

"Of course, I do. The only reason I was so upset about Anna was that she wasn't you. I didn't love her. I didn't even remember her, then suddenly she was there claiming to be pregnant with my baby. I was afraid that the baby that she claimed was mine, would ruin what we have. I don't want anything to mess up what we have but you being pregnant? Us having a baby together? None of that is going to ruin anything. It's only going to make our lives richer and more exciting, more fulfilled. I want to have a baby with you. I love you."

"I love you too."

CHAPTER 28

Mia was pregnant. I was going to be a father. The thought made me smile. But I needed to get Mia to the hospital to be checked out. I wanted to make sure that our baby was okay after such a rough landing.

The ambulance pulled up at the hospital and Mia and I were able to climb out on our own. We were led through the ambulance bay to a room filled with exam tables and thin curtains that wrapped around them for privacy.

"Here you are, madam. You'll be in bay seven and monsieur, we will put you in bay eight," the nurse said as he motioned toward the two cubicles.

"No. Absolutely not. We're not separating."

"The doctors must have their own space to examine each of you, monsieur. It will only be for a few minutes."

"Let me make myself crystal clear. I will not, under any circumstances, be taking my eyes off of her."

"How about we make a compromise?" One of the nurses came up from behind me and I turned to face her, all while still keeping Mia in my peripheral vision. The nurse flushed slightly and took a step back as I faced her. "I was just going to say," her voice was lower with my attention on her. "What if we open the curtain between the two rooms? That way it's pretty much like being in the same room but the doctors are able to have the space they need to examine you both."

"Yes. See, was that so hard?" I asked the first nurse and he seemed to visibly shrink back.

I didn't wait for them and pulled the curtain back myself as I stepped into the room. We were in a foreign country where our last name didn't hold as much weight as it did in other places. The people who did know who we were, were not all friendly. The Paris underworld was a place of tension for members of the Italian mafia. Though, I did have some associates in the area.

I struggled to keep my eyes on Mia as the doctor got in my way checking my pupils and reflexes. Once my exam was done, I rushed over to see how Mia was doing.

"How is she, Doc?"

"She appears in good health," the doctor said thoughtfully. "We're about to do an ultrasound to check on the little one."

I helped Mia lay back on the exam table and watched curiously as the doctor squeezed clear gel on her belly and began rubbing a small handheld device over her stomach. At first, there was just a strange, muffled sound but finally it cleared as the familiar rhythm of a heartbeat came through the machine.

"Strong heartbeat," the doctor confirmed.

"That's the baby's heartbeat?"

"It is."

I squeezed Mia's hand gently as I listened in awe.

"And if you look at the screen right there, that is your baby." The doctor pointed to a small bean shaped spot on the screen and I took a step closer to get a better look.

"That little thing?"

"Yes. But he or she will grow quickly. Actually, let me see..." The doctor started messing with the machine before talking again. "Three-point-four centimeters. Based on these measurements, it seems you're about ten weeks along."

"Ten week—" A flash of anger nearly blinded me as the sudden realization hit. "So you were pregnant when that bastard took you—" Mia squeezed my hand, glancing from me to the doctor and back, signaling for me not to say too much in front of regular civilians.

I took a deep breath and tried to calm my surging rage toward the man I had already killed. He had kidnapped not only my fiancée but unknowingly, my unborn child as well. I wished that I could bring him back to life just to be able to kill him again.

Mia gently squeezed my hand, grounding me, and I let out a breath.

The doctor cleared his throat. "Everything looks really good here. Mom and baby are both healthy."

"You're sure?"

"Yes. As sure as I can be right now."

"Right now? What do you mean as sure as you can be right now? What kind of doctor are you if you don't know for certain?"

"What I mean is, everything looks perfect right now, but you need to come back if there are any changes: spotting, pain, or just anything that makes you feel uncomfortable." The doctor made sure to look at Mia and not me. He was probably getting the idea that, if it were up to me, I'd have Mia in a private room, monitored twenty-four-seven, and with me constantly by her side.

"We will. Thank you, Doctor," Mia said before I had a chance to respond.

"Give me a few minutes and I will get your discharge papers ready along with the contact number that you can call in case you have any issues while you're here in Paris. I hear that you arrived with quite the dramatic flair on a private jet today."

"We did," I said, giving a little away.

"Well, I hope you enjoy your trip to Paris and that the rest of the trip is less eventful than your arrival."

"Thank you."

While the doctor worked on getting our discharge papers ready, I took the time to order us a rental car for the duration of our trip. I didn't have a regular car service in France. And after everything that had happened, I craved the control of driving myself and Mia wherever we needed to go.

Fifteen minutes later the nurse came back in with a stapled stack of papers and a couple of forms for us to sign.

We flipped through the packet as the nurse went over the release instructions. I got a confirmation text that our rental car was waiting out front for us, so we finished our paperwork and headed outside.

I helped Mia into her seat and rounded to the driver's side. "I need to make a quick call on our way to the hotel, then we can focus completely on us. I promise."

"Okay, but is everything alright?"

"You're safe, our baby is safe, nothing else matters."

"Don't forget...you're safe. That matters too."

I nodded instead of arguing the fact that I didn't matter nearly as much as they did, but I knew that Mia would just argue the point. I suppose to each of us, the other was the most important thing in the world. Except for that all changed, at least a little bit, the moment that Mia became pregnant.

I punched in a few numbers and docked my phone in the holder. Within two rings, Calabro, our pilot, answered. "*Buon pomeriggio, Signore Venturi.* Is everything alright?"

"*Sì.* Were you hurt in the landing?"

"No, *Signore.* The paramedics checked me out on the scene and cleared me to go have the plane looked at. How are you and *Signora* Venturi?"

"We're fine. What can you tell me about the plane?"

"There's the expected damage to the underbelly but nothing too substantial that it can't be fixed. Insurance should cover all the damages."

"What about the reason *why* the landing gear didn't deploy in the first place?"

"Oh, that I'm not sure of. There was nothing to indicate a problem before we took off. I reviewed the pre-flight report before we left."

"But you didn't do the inspection yourself?" I nearly growled the words as my hands tightened on the steering wheel.

"No, *Signore.* I had one of my men do it. All approved by your father, of course."

"I want the name of the technician who did the pre-flight check and I want you to do a personal inspection yourself to see if there was any sign of sabotage."

"You don't think it was a mistake? You think this was done on purpose?"

"I don't know but after everything that has happened lately, I wouldn't dismiss the possibility without a thorough investigation."

"Of course, *Signore*."

"And I want the results of your investigation first thing in the morning, earlier if you find something before then. It doesn't matter the time."

"*Sì, Signore.*" I ended the call and glanced over at Mia who sat looking at me with her brow raised.

"You think this was done on purpose? That someone tried to cause a crash?"

"I don't know. But we need to be sure. Until those fucking Corsicans and Romanos are taken care of, I won't ever trust that we'll be safe."

"Hopefully that will be soon. Have you heard anything from Alessandro or Luca yet?"

"Nothing definitive but they are safe and working on finding the men responsible for so much of your pain and suffering. I promise you, I will make this world safe for you and for our child."

I took Mia's hand and lifted it to my lips while glancing at her. She didn't look convinced of what I was saying. She looked worried and I couldn't blame her. I'd promised to keep her safe for months and failed to do so at every turn.

Once I got Mia back to the hotel, we ordered room service and stayed in, neither of us feeling like a night out after the day we'd had. After a long, warm shower, I led Mia to the bed, kissing her softly the whole way as I laid her down gently.

My mind drifted to that little life growing inside her and I gently ran my hand across her flat belly. She would be giving me the greatest gift anyone could ever give.

"That's my baby in there," I rasped, the words too full of emotion.

"It is." Mia smiled affectionately up at me, her hair sprawled around her on the pillow.

I leaned down, placing my lips just above the small strip of exposed skin between Mia's shirt and her panties. "*Ciao, tesorino*. I'm your papa."

"I don't think the baby can hear you this early on," Mia said but she was smiling down at me.

I kissed her belly, slowly moving up her body, leaving a trail of kisses behind until I reached her neck. I nipped and nibbled as I kissed up to her ear and she squirmed. My warm breath caressed her ear as I whispered in a gravelly tone, no longer hiding my need from her. "Good. Then they won't hear what I'm about to do to their mama."

I slipped my hand into her panties which were already wet. She moaned, her back arching with each skillful move. I strummed her body like a musician playing his favorite instrument, pulling each moan, each whimper, each cry of pleasure at my command. It was a powerful feeling to hold so much control over her body. To be able to give her so much pleasure after all the pain she'd had to endure. I swore to myself right then that I would do everything in my power to fill her life with only pleasure.

CHAPTER 29

Mia

Our first night in Paris hadn't gone the way either of us had planned, with a near plane crash and a trip to the emergency room. But I enjoyed the downtime just relaxing with Teo in our hotel.

I was awoken from a peaceful sleep by soft, gentle kisses on my neck. I moaned softly and my eyes fluttered open to see Teo gazing adoringly down at me.

"*Buongiorno.*" I smiled up at Teo.

"*Buongiorno bellezza.*" Teo gently brushed a strand of my hair from my face. "Did you sleep well?"

"I did. What's the plan for today?" I stretched and sat up in bed.

"Well I thought that we would go out for breakfast first if you're up for it." Teo looked at me expectantly.

"I think I need some ginger ale and crackers before I'm going to be able to get up and get ready to go anywhere. But usually once I get that in my system, it seems to get better and my appetite returns, too. So that sounds great."

"Good. Then I'll grab those from the mini bar. Then we can be on our way."

"Thank you." I smiled and Teo hurried over to the minibar to get a pack of crackers and the ginger ale from the fridge.

Once my morning sickness was under control, I was able to shower and get ready for our first full day in Paris. While Teo had been to Paris plenty of times in the past, I had never been. I was always focused on my studies and my father was very protective, so we didn't travel outside of Italy very often. I was excited to see all the famous places in Paris.

Although we had missed our first day, it seemed Teo was making up for lost time. We started our morning at a charming little outdoor café which had the most delicious crepes and amazing coffee, then a stroll through the park. After that, Teo took me back to the hotel for lunch and a nap.

I woke up with my head on Teo's chest. I forced my heavy eyes open to find him just lying there, staring down at me, and he brushed my hair back from my face.

"How long have you been awake?"

"I never slept. I just enjoyed watching you."

"That's either very romantic or very creepy," I teased.

"I suppose it depends on the context."

"I believe so."

"And in this context?" Teo lifted his brow playfully.

"We'll go with romantic."

"Good. And there is more romance where that came from."

"Planning on staring at me some more?" I smirked, lifting my head to see him better.

"I planned on taking you on a sunset cruise down the River Seine. You can see so much of the city that way. I thought it would be a good introduction to the city and we could talk about all the things you want to do while we are here."

"That sounds wonderful."

"Are you sure? Because if you'd rather me just stare at you..." Teo teased.

"No, no, no. That sounds amazing. I'd love that."

"Good. Now, before we go, there is one thing that we need to take care of."

"What's that?"

Teo moved quickly and before I knew what was happening, my back was against the mattress with Teo on top, pinning me to the bed. My soft giggles were cut off as he kissed me deep and hard.

He let his hands roam over my body, igniting every nerve ending, warming my skin with his tender touch until I was writhing underneath him, desperate with need.

He slowly slipped my shirt over my head, kissing the newly exposed flesh as he peeled each piece of fabric from my body until I lay bare before him. Teo had never been so gentle and while I loved every side of him, the excruciatingly slow way he slid inside me, lit my whole body on fire.

"You feel amazing," Teo growled in my ear and I moaned.

My hips lifted to meet his every thrust and I reached up, gripping his back and pulling him down onto me, needing to feel him covering my body. I wanted to feel every inch of him.

Pleasure built so intense that I thought I might explode. I gripped Teo's shoulders, my nails catching his skin and he surged forward, deeper into me.

My body shattered, clenching tight around his cock as I clawed his back. I cried out from the intensity of my release and Teo swallowed my cries with his kiss.

As the waves of ecstasy subsided, Teo collapsed beside me, both of us panting for air. We didn't move to get up for several minutes.

Teo was the first to move, lifting me from the bed and carrying me to the shower. It was everything we could do not to devour each other all over again but Teo warned that if we did, we'd miss our cruise.

The sunset along the River Seine was amazing. We sat at our table, eating a delicious meal as all the best sites of Paris passed by.

Teo moved his chair to sit beside me, pointing out all of the main Parisian attractions. "If you look right over there…" Teo leaned over and pointed at a large building. "That is the Louvre. I was thinking tomorrow we could go there for a tour and maybe catch a show at the Moulin Rouge after dinner."

"You really have put a lot of thought into this."

"Oh, absolutely," Teo practically purred as he leaned closer. "I want to spoil you with every indulgence."

He placed his hand on my leg, under the table. My dress rode up so that his fingers brushed against the tender, bare flesh, and I sucked in a quick breath, so affected by even the smallest touch from him.

"You're too good to me." My words came out breathy as his hand slipped under my dress and began moving higher until he was barely an inch from the apex of my thighs.

"Just making up for all I've put you through."

"You didn't—"

"Still. Just let me spoil you." He slipped a finger under the lace fabric of my panties and brushed against my dampened mound.

"Teo," I breathed out while glancing around at the other tables filled with people. "Someone will see."

"No one is going to notice as long as you sit still and keep quiet."

He slipped a finger inside my wet folds and I gasped, biting my lip to stay quiet. "Teo…"

"Shh," he softly shushed me, leaning in so that his warm breath tickled my ear. "Already so wet for me."

He moved his finger, excruciatingly slow at first but quickly built up his tempo as he slid another thick digit inside. I gasped and squirmed in my seat. I glanced around, half expecting everyone on the boat to be staring at us but everyone was too taken in by the views of the city.

"Teo…please?" I wasn't sure if I was begging him to stop or to keep going but he quickened his pace.

Teo thrust his fingers harder and faster. I gripped the edge of the table, trying to force myself to stay still when all I wanted to do was buck my hips and take him deeper. My body was wound as tight as a spring, coiled and ready to burst yet Teo didn't relent.

"Teo…" I warned as I neared climax.

"Shh. Hold on for just a moment longer, *bellissima*."

We neared another bridge. As per custom, everyone began cheering as the boat swept under the bridge and with perfect timing, Teo sent me over the edge. White lights exploded behind my eyes, and I bit my lip hard to keep from crying out.

As we emerged from the other side of the bridge, Teo withdrew his fingers, and pulled me close. I sagged against him, panting as my heart hammered against my chest. Teo just looked down at me with a satisfied smirk.

After our cruise, we took advantage of the beautiful night, strolling along the city streets and taking in all the lights of the city.

I tried to hide my yawn as I grew sleepy. The pregnancy seemed to take a lot of my energy.

"Seems like I need to get you to bed."

"I'm sorry. Who knew a little tiny peanut of a baby could be this exhausting?"

We turned down a small, quiet side street toward the hotel when another pedestrian bumped into me. I startled but when I went to jump back, I realized he had a grip on my arm and his hand tightened around my bicep.

Teo whirled around just as the man tugged me against him with my back to his chest, his forearm across my neck, and a knife in his hand.

"Don't try anything," the man warned. "Empty out your pockets. Wallet, money clip, watch...put it all in the lady's purse." He gave me a little squeeze. "Go ahead, pretty thing, hold your bag out for him."

"Teo..." I trembled but did my best to remain calm and held my purse out as I locked eyes with Teo.

"It's okay. Everything's going to be okay." Teo kept his gaze set on me as he slowly pulled out his wallet and stuck it in my purse. He unfastened his watch and slipped it into my bag as well.

He moved slowly with smooth motions that spoke to his steel nerves while I trembled like a leaf in a strong breeze.

For the first time, Teo's eyes flicked down to the man's arm across my neck and there was a flash of worry in his eyes that made me panic. Teo was always so confident, anything less was usually cause for concern.

"Alright, I'm going to reach for my money clip," Teo spoke in a calm voice, though there was something that made me nervous in his eyes.

He slowly reached into the inner pocket of his blazer and pulled out a gold money clip with a thick wad of euro notes. Teo's chest rose and fell with a deep breath as he slowly extended his hand toward my hand bag. He dropped the money inside but instead of pulling his hand back, he moved it up at lightning speed.

Everything moved so quickly that I hardly knew what was happening until I was standing behind Teo who had our assailant pinned to the brick wall of the alley with his arm pinned behind his back. The man's knife was discarded on the ground, and Teo pressed his gun to the man's temple.

"Who sent you? Tell me who sent you," Teo roared at the man who winced at the barrel of the gun pressing into his temple.

"What the fuck are you talking about?"

"Tell me who sent you." Teo wrenched the man's arm back further and he hissed through his teeth.

"Nobody sent me."

"Bullshit. You're with the Corsicans."

"Yeah, so?"

252

Teo started to pull back on the man's arm again but paused. "You feel that pain? That pull? All I need is one swift motion and it's torn from the socket so you better start giving me answers."

"Okay, I'll tell you anything you want to know, just please, please let go."

"After you start talking."

"Man, the Corsicans will *kill* me for talking," he whined.

"And if you don't start, I'm going to make you *wish* you were dead."

Teo pulled up slightly on the arm and the guy cried out. I winced just imagining the pain, and looked around, hoping that no one heard. They'd never believe that Teo and I had been the victims.

"Okay! I'm just a new recruit. I've only been with them for a few months. I'm still earning my place, so I get money by robbing tourists."

"Then how did you just happen to pick us?"

"I don't even know who you are. I just saw the two of you, distracted by each other, wearing your fancy clothes. I figured it would be an easy score."

"You were wrong about that."

"Yeah, I see that."

"So that's it? You just so happened to pick us off the streets?"

"Yeah, I don't know you from Adam, I swear."

"Alright. Okay…" Teo relaxed the pressure on the man's arm and he winced. Teo kept him pinned to the wall, even as he bent down to retrieve the man's knife. "I am going to hold on to this, though. To make sure you don't turn around and use it on me."

"Oh, I'd never try that again. I learned my lesson, honestly, I have. But you can keep the knife. It's yours."

"Good," Teo said decisively.

Without releasing the man, Teo reached around and dragged the knife's blade deep across his throat. I threw a hand over my mouth to fight back a scream of both surprise and horror. The man's cries came out as nothing more than a gargle as blood splattered the brick wall. Teo released him, and his body crumpled to the ground.

My knees went weak, and I had to lean against the opposite wall to hold myself up. Teo ran over to me and wrapped an arm around my waist.

"Are you okay?"

"I think I'm going to be sick."

"Not here. We can't leave any evidence of us behind. Look away, try to breathe, if you have to throw up, go to the main street, right around the corner, there were some planters there. I just need a minute.

I nodded, unable to speak without risking throwing up. I turned my back on the gruesome scene and reached into my purse that still hung, nearly forgotten on my arm, and dug out a peppermint to help settle my stomach.

Teo wiped his fingerprints off of the knife using the man's shirt and dropped it beside him before returning to me.

"Okay, let's get out of here." Teo wrapped one arm around me for support and I caught a glimpse of the red, staining his other hand.

"Teo," I paused my steps before we made it onto the main street. "Your hand."

He quickly shoved his hand in his jacket pocket to hide the blood and hurried me along toward the hotel.

Once we were safely back in the room with our door locked, Teo stripped out of his jacket and shirt. He cleaned the blood from his hands while I stood in the doorway staring, still half in shock.

"Teo?"

"Yes? Are you okay?" He glanced up at me in the bathroom mirror before drying his hands and hurrying to my side.

I nodded but I wasn't sure if it was a lie or not.

Teo led me to sit on the edge of the bed and took a seat beside me.

"Why did you kill that man? He seemed legitimately scared. Do you think that he would have actually turned around and hurt us after all that?"

"He may very well have been scared. Many men are when they think they might die. But he was not just some new recruit."

"How do you know?"

"The tattoo on his hand. The four dots."

"What does that mean?"

"It's a tattoo given by Graziani, the leader of the Corsicans that we ran into in Nice. You see, there is a common French prison tattoo that is five dots, four in a square, one in the middle. It signifies a man who has done time. The four walls and the man inside, but Graziani's men make a point to never be taken alive. Always leaving the prison cells empty."

"The four walls, no one inside," I said, following along.

"Exactly. He had the mark on his hand. That's how I knew that he wasn't just some street thug. Graziani only gives those tattoos to men who have earned it."

"Wow. Okay." My shoulders slumped with some relief that Teo had had a good reason for killing that man. I should have known by that point that I could trust him not to act rashly or to be unnecessarily cruel.

"I'm very sorry that you had to see that, especially considering everything." Teo reached down and gently placed his hand on my belly.

Just because I'm pregnant doesn't mean that I'm made of glass."

"I know that, but I never want you to have to experience the darker parts of our world. I wish I could shield both of you from all of it."

"How is this going to work? Raising a baby in the life that we live. Keeping our child safe from enemies..." I said more as a question to myself than to Teo but he answered anyway.

"We protect him or her the same way that our parents protected us. By working to bring more and more power to our family, more respect, more security. We strive to become untouchable so that our children and their children's children will continue to be safe for decades to come."

Teo wrapped his arms around me, enveloping me in his warm embrace and I breathed in the comforting scent of him, feeling safe in the arms of the man I love, my husband.

CHAPTER 30

Teo

With the exception of a few bumps in the road, Mia and I had really enjoyed Paris. I'd been a fool to agree to take her to France knowing the stronghold that the Corsicans maintained there but when Mia had told me she'd always wanted to go but had never had the chance, I knew that I had to do that for her.

I couldn't imagine one thing on God's green earth that I would deny that woman. I just had to hope that she didn't realize just how wrapped around her finger I'd become.

With the jet still under repair, we took a commercial plane home, figuring that would be safer than chartering a private jet that the Corsicans might try to sabotage. They wouldn't dare attempt something like that on a commercial flight for fear of shining too big of a spotlight on their organization.

Fausto insisted on being the one to pick us up from the airport. Mia was happy to see him since he hadn't been around as much since he started helping run our joint family security. Mia and I both trusted him, and his military experience plus two decades serving as security for the Monticelli's made him the perfect man for the job.

We pulled onto the road that led to the compound when Fausto slowed down.

"There's something you two should know."

I tensed, not liking the tone of his voice, and Mia sat up straighter. "What is it?"

"There was an incident while you were away."

"What kind of incident?"

"A bombing—it never made it to the house. The guards' house took the brunt of the blast, but we lost two men."

"*Shit.*"

Fausto glanced in the rearview mirror. "I wanted to tell you right away. I didn't like keeping it from you but Don Venturi said he didn't want to ruin your honeymoon over something you couldn't do anything about. He said you'd be don when you got back but until then, he'd handle it."

"How did the bomb get on the property?" I asked angrily though it wasn't directed at Fausto but at the ones responsible.

259

"It came in as a wedding gift. Security missed it. That's my fault and I take full responsibility."

"No. It was an accident. If you missed it then I have no doubt that everything was done to try to prevent it from happening."

"Thank you, *Signore*."

We pulled onto the winding drive that led to the gate. Construction equipment surrounded three sides of the rubble that once was the guard house and the reality of how much we could have lost hit me hard. "*Fuck*. They weren't messing around."

"No, *Signore*. We found two others in the process of sorting through gifts. All different types of explosives with different triggers. I guess they wanted to ensure one of them made it through."

"I will be so glad when Alessandro and Luca finally take down Graziani once and for all. I just hate that I won't be the one to put a bullet in his head."

Mia squeezed my hand and I looked at her, my expression softening.

Fausto pulled up to the front of the house and put the car in park before rounding the car to open it for Mia.

Two other men hurried out of the house to get our bags while Mia and I headed inside.

We were greeted by an extremely excited Lucia and Bianca who stood in the foyer, waiting for us to arrive.

"*Benvenuto a casa*," Bianca called out excitedly as she kissed both of my cheeks, then Mia's, and Lucia did the same.

260

"Your father is in the parlor waiting for you."

"Excellent. Thank you." Mia and I walked to the parlor to find my father.

"Ah, if it isn't our future don returning from his honeymoon." He grinned and sat his drink on the table before standing to greet us.

Another man close to the same age and build who had been sitting with him stood as well.

"I would like to introduce both of you both to Don Costa." My father motioned toward the distinguished looking man beside him.

The name sounded familiar but I couldn't quite place it.

"A pleasure." I held out my hand and he shook it firmly.

"Likewise. And congratulations on your recent nuptials. I heard it was no easy feat, making it down the aisle."

"It was a bit challenging," Mia added.

"Those damned Corsicans have got some nerve. The Romanos, too. Despicable, the kind of tactics they stooped to." I studied Costa, wondering where I knew the name from and why he was in my home but I wouldn't dare ask him and insult him. Not with him being my father's guest.

"Well, we don't want to interrupt. I just wanted to let you know that we are home."

"Please, have a drink with us? We were just discussing the potential for joining our families."

Costa's words slammed into me like a brick, and I struggled to remain stoic and keep my tone even. "Join families?"

I looked from Costa to my father for clarification and he nodded. "As my last act as don before I pass that title over to you tomorrow, Costa and I have arranged a very advantageous marriage."

"I do believe that your daughter will enjoy Sicily."

"Mira?" I asked in shock and looked between the two men. "Papa, can I speak with you for a moment?"

"Don't be rude, my son. Pour yourself a drink and sit for a while."

"I thought that Mira was going to be the family lawyer." I tried to appear unfazed so to hide my worry, I walked to the bar and poured myself a glass of bourbon and Mia a glass of club soda.

"She is but she's also going to be the donna of the Costa family."

"Mira will never agree to this," Mia whispered to me the same sentiment I was already thinking.

"Can I please speak with you alone for a moment?" I couldn't hide the desperation in my voice as I practically begged for a private audience with my father.

"I already understand that your sister is a modern woman, strong willed, and independent. But I do believe that she will be happy with my son. And Stefano will certainly be happy with such an impressive wife."

"Pardon my frankness. It's nothing personal. Your son could be a crowned prince and Mira would still not be okay with being in an arranged marriage."

"I believe you misunderstand our intent. We aren't going to force the two together. We are just going to encourage the relationship and in the event that they hit it off, we will have a good base for a prenuptial agreement."

"I see." I was still hesitant to put much faith in the arrangement working out.

Costa's phone chimed and he pulled it from his pocket just long enough to glance at it before slipping back.

"I'm afraid I should be getting back home but it was good speaking with you, Piero, and a pleasure to meet the two of you."

"Likewise." I forced a smile and waited for him to leave before letting my indifferent mask fall as I turned to look at my father who was calmly sipping his scotch. "You know that Mira will never go for this."

"I'm only asking her to give him a chance. Just a few dates. From there, we will see how it goes."

I shook my head, trying to calm my anger, knowing how Mira would feel about the whole thing. She loved my father and would want to do anything to make him happy. But she was a strong woman and I couldn't see her agreeing to any of it.

"Come, it's just about time for dinner. I want to hear all about your trip."

Mia glanced at me and I smiled at her, gently squeezing her thigh before we stood to follow my father to the dining room.

"I asked Bianca to make one of your favorites." My father grinned as we took our seats.

Bianca and Lucia came out to bring the wine and first course. When Lucia went to fill Mia's glass, Mia placed her hand over the glass. "None for me tonight, thank you."

"No wine?" My father glanced up curiously. Mia tensed and looked at me.

Excitement bubbled up in my chest, the conversation from before pushed to the back of my mind, and I gave Mia a nod of encouragement.

"Well, actually..." Mia hesitated.

"We have some news," I finished her sentence and gave her a nod to continue.

"News?" My father's tone lifted, sounding hopeful and I knew he'd already figured it out or at the very least, had a pretty good guess as to what it was.

"I'm pregnant," Mia announced happily.

All formality was lost as Lucia practically squealed and hugged Mia. My father stood and embraced me.

"You're going to be a father," he said proudly. "Congratulations, my son. Congratulations to both of you." He hurried over to Mia and gave her a hug as well. I laughed as she looked slightly flustered by the act of affection from my usually stoic father but the news was cause for celebration.

"We need to call your brother and sister," my father said excitedly.

Just then, my phone rang and I pulled it out. "This is Alessandro."

"Take it. We'll call Nic and Mira after." My father turned to Mia and as I stepped out of the door I smiled as I overheard him say, "now, if it's a boy, you're going to name him after me, right?"

I swiped the button on my phone to answer. "Hello?"

"Teo?" Alessandro's voice came through.

"Yeah."

"We got him. We got the bastard and his men. Took them out while they were at their meeting so we were able to get them all at once."

"That's fantastic."

"There's been no sign of Domenico, though."

"He probably slithered back home like the snake that he is."

"If he was ever even in Corsica. He could have been calling the shots from his papa's plush mansion for all we know."

"Either way, this news couldn't have come at a better time. Thank you, my friend."

"Trust me, I was happy to do it. Has there still been no word on Gabe?"

"None. We've got people watching his wife in case he tries to reach out, though."

"We'll find him eventually." I nodded to myself at his words.

"Do you need transport home?"

"No. We've got a cargo ship. We're heading that way now."

"Any casualties on our side?"

"Two of my guys," his voice deflated slightly at the mention of the loss. "Luca lost three of his men and a bullet grazed him as well."

"Luca was shot?"

"He assured me that it was just a flesh wound and that it could wait until we get back on Italian soil. He's more concerned for the fallen men."

"Their sacrifice was not in vain. You guys took out a huge enemy today and I will see that their families are taken care of."

"I know they will appreciate that."

"Make sure that Luca gets checked out as soon as you're home."

"I will. We should be offloading around Tuscany."

"Call me with your coordinates and I'll have the jet ready to transport you all as soon as you land. It should be patched up by then."

"Oh yeah, I heard about your dramatic entrance into France."

"You have no idea, but we will catch up on all of that as soon as you're back."

"I look forward to sitting down with you and having a strong drink after this."

"You got it."

I ended the call just as Mia joined me outside of the dining room. "Everything okay?"

"Better than okay." I slipped my arm around her and pulled her against me, dipping my head to softly kiss her lips. "They got them."

"What?" Mia looked up at me in surprise and confusion.

"Alessandro and Luca. They got Graziani and his men. Took them all out at a family meeting. It's over."

"Oh, Teo." Mia squeezed me tight and I tipped her chin up to claim her lips again.

"I told you we'd get them. We will take down anyone who threatens our family, and I will keep our baby safe. I promise you that."

"I love you," Mia whispered against my lips.

"I love you too, *bellissima*. With my whole heart."

NIKKI ROSE

ABOUT THE AUTHOR

For as long as she can remember, Nikki Rose has enjoyed writing stories. For years, writing was just a hobby for this South Carolina native. It was a way to let out all the stories floating around in her head. After one of those stories took on a mind of its own, outgrowing even the parameters of a single book, Rose knew she had to pursue her dream.

Married to her high school sweetheart and best friend, Rose feels she is truly living out a romance story of her very own. As a stay-at-home mom of two, she is blessed with the time needed to work on her writing career full-time while her kids are at school or in the wee hours while normal people sleep. She considers herself a music obsessed chocoholic and hopeless romantic who enjoys weaving romance stories with a healthy dose of mystery and suspense.

NIKKI ROSE

Other Books by Nikki Rose

The Line Series

Crossing the Line

Blurring the Line

Drawing the Line

Walking the Line

———

When Dae Breaks

When Knight Falls

———

Dangerous Games

Faceless

Forgotten Evil

———

Venturi Mafia Series

*See front matter for complete list

Made in the USA
Las Vegas, NV
29 January 2025

17195102R00163